THE
CONQUEST
OF THE EAST

Dr R. Durgadoss (his associates call him Dr DD) is an entrepreneur, an inspirational speaker, a writer and a life coach. He holds a PhD in corporate finance and has had a career spanning more than three decades with leading multinational institutions.

R. Durgadoss has a deep-rooted passion for Indian mythology, history and philosophy. Since his childhood, he could attract a number of followers with his mesmerizing storytelling capabilities.

Having held audiences spellbound with his powerful storytelling style during his lectures in various international forums, R. Durgadoss thought it was time for him to focus on a series in the historical/mythological fiction genre. *The Conquest of the East* is the third book of the series.

R. Durgadoss has styled himself as a motivator for Generation Next. He is keen on bringing out the unbreakable spirit of those who brave severe circumstances and dream big to display commendable courage. He currently lives with his family in Dubai.

To know more about the author and his other interesting works, you may log on to:

Facebook: https://www.facebook.com/DrDurgadoss/
Twitter: https://twitter.com/DrDurgadoss
Linkedin: http://www.linkedin.com/pub/dr-r-durgadoss-aiyer/ 11/b72/294
Website: http://www.drdd.co.in
Youtube: http://www.youtube.com/DurgadossAiyer
Google Plus: https://plus.google.com/107697928973372364348

Also by the author

The Indus Challenge 2016

THE CONQUEST OF THE EAST

ROYAL CROWN RETURNS

R. DURGADOSS
With
PADMANABH DIWANJI

RUPA

Published by
Rupa Publications India Pvt. Ltd 2018
7/16, Ansari Road, Daryaganj
New Delhi 110002

Sales centres:
Allahabad Bengaluru Chennai
Hyderabad Jaipur Kathmandu
Kolkata Mumbai

Copyright © R. Durgadoss 2018

All rights reserved.
No part of this publication may be reproduced, transmitted,
or stored in a retrieval system, in any form or by any means, electronic,
mechanical, photocopying, recording or otherwise, without the prior permission
of the publisher.

This is a work of fiction. Names, characters, places and incidents
are either the product of the author's imagination or are used
fictitiously and any resemblance to any actual person, living or dead,
events or locales is entirely coincidental and is not intended to hurt any
segment of our society. The author does not claim the accuracy of the
mythological/historical information used in this work.

ISBN: 978-93-5333-260-0

First impression 2018

10 9 8 7 6 5 4 3 2 1

The moral right of the author has been asserted.

Printed by Parksons Graphics Pvt. Ltd., Mumbai

This book is sold subject to the condition that it shall not,
by way of trade or otherwise, be lent, resold, hired out, or otherwise circulated,
without the publisher's prior consent, in any form of binding or cover other
than that in which it is published.

To Emperor Rajendra Chola, South India's Alexander and his generals, who braved severe circumstances yet dared to dream big...

Contents

Introduction: Janam Three	ix
Prologue	xxi
Part I: The Birth in a Sacred Bath	1
Part II: The Adoption of the Orphan Surya	15
Part III: The Beginning of Surya's Royal Connection	23
Part IV: Surya: The Royal Navy Commander	41
Part V: The Lanka Expedition	81
Part VI: The Ganga Expedition	101
Part VII: The Love That Blossomed	153
Part VIII: The Srivijaya Expedition	181
Part IX: Return to the Capital	193
Epilogue	226
Acknowledgements	227
Glossary	229

Introduction: Janam Three

Recap...
Track Travelled So Far...

Janam One: The Shackles of the Warrior
2008

A terrorist group attacks the world by planting viruses into global computer systems through a satellite orbiting the earth. This act of cyberterrorism disrupts air traffic systems, interferes with the control systems for water and electricity, blocks commercial communications, crashes various network systems, gains access to secret military information and defaces websites. In light of this cyberattack, the world is facing a chaotic situation.

Shiv, a young, celebrated NASA scientist, destroys the group's moves and saves the earth from cyberattacks. To honour Shiv's extraordinary performance, a felicitation function is held at the Taj Mahal Palace Hotel, Mumbai, on the fateful day of 26 November 2008. Shiv, the cyberwarrior, becomes a victim of the terrorist attack at the Taj Mahal. His mind flashes with several images while he lies in a coma in the ICU of a leading hospital in Mumbai. The images of war, weapons and weeping widows swamp his mind. Are these flashes from his previous births?

3000 BC

The hero who saved the planet from cyberterrorists could not avoid succumbing to this physical terrorism. Shiv's unconscious mind questioned: Why?

The memories from his time in a coma were inexplicable. They were like a patchwork quilt, with no apparent sequence nor temporal relationship with one another. The purest and the most extraordinary part of his journey had commenced deep in his state of coma. In the midst of his coma, his cerebrum unleashed a quest to unravel his past. Then, all of a sudden, everything opened up. His mind entered a valley, so beautiful that he could see with clarity.

He could see waterfalls, pools of water, and indescribable colours with arcs of silver and gold light, and beautiful hymns emanating from them. Boom! Suddenly, the serene image shifted into images of war, weapons and weeping widows. He saw himself on the mast of a tall ship, he saw himself in a missile silo, and he saw himself on the watchtower of a mammoth fort, and then guiding the cannons of a great warship. And then he saw images of himself move out of the earth and the universe. He had lost awareness of his own body during his coma. In the process of this search, his mind realized many of his previous states, breaking the shackles of all his earlier births.

His mind was filled with the chorus of a great army crying out the name, 'Sagar, Sagar, Sagar…' He was lying on a battlefield, a wounded soldier covered with deep cuts. It was a bloodbath all around.

He was holding back his last breath, waiting for his beloved wife and newborn son. It was the battle between the Kauravas and the Pandavas, in the land situated between the two rivers, the Saraswati and Drishadvati, the land where Manu wrote his Manusmriti, and the land where the Rig and Sama Vedas were compiled.

His calm mind resisted the image. 'This battleground is not the land of my birth or my beloved kingdom. This is not the place where I spent my joyful childhood. This is not the beautiful place where I come from. I need to find the place of my birth.'

His comatose mind continued to wander further into the past. It now flashed images of the spectacular city of his birth. The golden fort of this city threw its glitter on the surrounding waters, making it look like as though flames were rising from the riverbed. There was a township with six sectors along the banks of the river. It was connected to the mainland via floating bridges, which could be withdrawn whenever there was an attack. The floating bridges and the design of the city were marvellous.

Having identified the city of his birth, he stumbled onto his colourful life as Sagar, the great warrior of the kingdom of Krishna in 3083 BC.

Sagar, in his first karmic avatar, was given the Shudra Varna tag but was patronized by a Brahmin guru. He was given the status of a Shudra by society, but the status of a strategic warrior by his leader, Abhimanyu.

Sagar grew up with three Brahmin friends (the sons of his guruji), the Kshatriya leader Abhimanyu and another friend who was a Vaishya. A close bond developed among all of them at the gurukul.

The three sons of his guruji were also blessed with mystic powers. All the pancha bhootas—earth, water, sky, air and fire—danced to the tunes of the three boys who were born as triplets. All of them were more or less the same age as Sagar.

One boy was extraordinarily proficient in earth-related matters. He knew the topography, water bodies, likelihood of an earthquake and how to create tremors in the earth. He could identify the movement of creatures beneath the ground. He could create a hole, go into the earth and come out of another place by navigating the surface below. He could stay beneath the earth for months without anyone knowing about it. When he fought on earth, no one could conquer him.

The second boy was blessed with extraordinary powers underwater. He could swim below the water, stay under it for ages, invoke hard varuna (water) and bring rain at will. When he fought on water, no one could conquer him.

The third boy was highly talented in matters of the sky. He could invoke vayu (air), change the direction of the wind, speak to birds and talk to people in far-off places through air. When he fought from a height, no one could defeat him.

But the pancha bhootas would only obey them when the three of them were together. They were warned of a threat to their lives at the age of fifteen. As they grew older, they joined Abhimanyu's Yuva Sena.

Sagar was the chief strategist of the Yuva Sena, marshalling resources for his leader Abhimanyu. During the Kuru War, on the fateful day of the chakravyuha, Sagar was advised by his guruji that he should not send his three gifted sons to the field. According to their horoscopes, their lives were under threat.

But fate took the decision away from him.

A nine-layer chakravyuha had been formed by Guru Drona. All of Duryodana's greatest warriors were in the inner circle while the outer circle was protected by the mighty Drona. The Pandava warrior Arjuna, the only one who knew how to cleave the chakravyuha, had been dragged off to a different field. Now, the onus of breaking the chakravyuha fell upon the young Abhimanyu, Arjuna's son. He knew how to break in the chakravyuha but he did not know how to exit.

The Yuva Sena volunteered to enter the chakravyuha, assigning the seniors the task of ensuring that the breach remained open to allow for a clear line of retreat. A contingency plan was made.

Chakravyuha entrance

The three Brahmin boys' powers would be used to create an underground tunnel through each tier, so that the soldiers would be able to retreat in case anything went wrong. A portion of the army could also use the tunnels so that they could be shielded from arrows while moving ahead and defending the broken edges of the tier. Also, even if the tiers were closed due to any reason, the mouths of the tunnels would provide a ready exit for Abhimanyu.

The innovative tactic of outsmarting the chakravyuha by using the mystical powers of the Sena brothers, was deliberated upon in the strategy discussions, held during the early meetings.

When the Yuva Sena was ready to enter the chakravyuha, one of the southern kings supporting the Pandavas thundered:

'How do you expect my forces to be led by a Shudra? It's not possible. I will not allow this.'

Abhimanyu and Sagar were hurt. They knew that time was being wasted. The arrangement of forces to counter the chakravyuha would take at least half a nazhiga (one nazhiga equals twenty-four minutes as a day is divided into sixty nazhigas). Abhimanyu asked Sagar to stay silent and stated that he would explain the situation. But no one was listening to him. As the talks went on between Abhimanyu and the southern kings, an emissary arrived with a message, stating that Sagar's wife had given birth to a boy.

Abhimanyu wanted Sagar to be with his wife, see his son and come back. In the meantime, he would make the arrangements for the army. But the southern kings were adamant. They would not fight under a Shudra. Exasperated, Abhimanyu and Sagar gave up. Abhimanyu instructed Sagar to go back and be with his wife. He asked one of the southern kings to be the rearguard instead.

Sagar said to Abhimanyu, 'I do not know whether to be happy for my son or sad that on the eve of the battle, I cannot be with you.'

Abhimanyu replied, 'Keep the sweets ready. I will come back and we will celebrate the birth of your son.'

Sagar went to his Brahmin friends and said, 'You should be very careful. Stay with Abhimanyu at all times. As long as you are with Abhimanyu, I will not be afraid. Also, under no circumstances should you get separated. Stay together and ride together.'

Sagar left the battlefield with a feeling of guilt, afraid that he was leaving the three boys and foregoing his guruji's strict instructions.

In the meantime, Abhimanyu's young blood and the heat of the battle overtook him. He fought alone like a warrior who does not value his own life. He started to move further ahead while his army, which could not match his swiftness, began to fall back. All his uncles were stuck far behind near the first tier of the chakravyuha.

His rearguard was pursued and attacked by Drona. The three Brahmin boys with special powers were separated in the subsequent melee which took place. Since they were separated, they could not invoke the pancha bhootas as their mystic skills only worked when they were together. Plans for the tunnel were turned to dust and with them went the last ray of hope for a safe return.

Moreover, the strategic master Sagar, who channellized their mystic powers into a coordinated strategy, was not there with them. Hence, each one of them became a powerless island, lending no assistance with their supernatural abilities.

The senior Pandavas were held back at the entrance of the chakravyuha while the circles of the chakravyuha were closed by their opponents leaving the Yuva Sena boys—Abhimanyu and the three Brahmin boys—stuck inside different tiers. After a valiant battle, the soul of the young hero Abhimanyu departed this world, unsatisfied. He had bravely fought to the best of his abilities. Had his opponents been honourable, and if he had more time, he would have surely destroyed all of them. Drona was satisfied, as he had struck a blow that would hurt the Pandavas. The chakravyuha had served its purpose.

Among the thousands who died on that day were the three Brahmin boys. Not being able to evoke their mystical powers, they lay dead in different tiers within the chakravyuha.

Sagar had been betrayed by his Vaishya wife. She had married him while pretending to love him, while in fact she desired to take revenge on him thinking that his Shudra father had been the cause of her father's death. She had unveiled their secret plan for the chakravyuha to the enemy, which brought complete havoc on the Yuva Sena warriors—including Abimanyu and the three Brahmin boys.

Sagar spoke of the tragedy to his guruji, who was meditating across the river. He roared, 'Sagar, I told you not to send my three sons to the war, as they had to suffer from a life threat at the age of fifteen. You promised to protect them. You are responsible for this. You knew they were blessed children. They were supposed to be extraordinary warriors on land, sea and air, supported by all the pancha bhootas. You shortened their lives. They might have lived at least three times longer. The story of their lives will always be that of success, and incompleteness. You have nipped their lives in the bud by not sticking to your word.

'I hereby curse you. You will live the forty-five years of each of my sons' remaining lives. But you will not live it in full. You will have the capability of each of my sons and like them, you will also die at the age of fifteen. Thus, you will take three births for each of my sons. You will take nine incarnations after this birth.

'You will be highly competent on land, sea and air matters in each of the three births. You can win a war but you cannot avail the fruits of it. Let these nine births forever remind you that you killed my sons in the nine-tier chakravyuha. Each of the nine circles will represent one birth for you. This is my curse. And yet, my anger is not slaked.'

Sagar was stunned. He could not understand how quickly his fate could turn around. His guru, the one who had almost adopted him, who was equal to his own father and had been everything to him, had turned against him.

He is a true Brahmin, and his curse will force me to face miseries in my subsequent births, he thought.

He pleaded with his guru, saying that he was not the only cause behind the death of his sons. He explained how circumstances such as the birth of his son and the revolt of the southern kings had prohibited him from participating in the battle on that day. But his guru did not reply to him, did not bother to listen to him and turned away.

Later, as he lay on his deathbed the next day, Sagar learned the secrets of his birth in a Kshatriya family and also about the betrayal of his wife.

He pleaded with his guruji on his deathbed.

'Guruji, I was penalized as a low caste Shudra even though I was born a Kshatriya; I was penalized by my wife for a cause to which my family and I were not a party; I was penalized by you for the death of your sons for which I was not the cause.

'I do not know why I have been singled out by my fate and punished for no fault of mine. But, I will not curse my fate, I lived true to the people around me, I was passionate in whatever I was doing, and I am willing to accept the results as they unfold. I truly believe that I have had to chase my goals but at the same time, I have had to learn to face the results. My only wish is that no one on earth be denied opportunities on grounds of his caste, creed or colour.

'Life may crown a person or make him a beggar on the streets. But no one should deprive anyone else of opportunities. Everyone should have equal opportunities. From below the ground comes a diamond; from the mud comes the lotus. Greatness can come from anyone. One's mother's womb should not determine one's destiny. I am saying this after facing troubles from the womb to my tomb. This is my death wish, Guruji,' Sagar concluded.

Bharadwaj had tears in his eyes, 'My dear Sagar, you speak like a philosopher. You have matured beyond your age. In the philosophy sessions at the gurukul, I saw the sparks in you. Today, I am seeing those sparks flare into flames. I have to correct myself. I gave you a curse of having a short life in your nine future births.

'I cannot take back my curse, and the arrow once out of the bow cannot be retrieved. I have no powers to withdraw it, but I can soften the curse. For each of the nine births to follow, I double your years from fifteen to thirty in each of the nine births. That is the best I can do, Sagar. But in every one of your births you will have a great impact on society. In three of your births, you will have special powers regarding land, the next three you will have special powers over water and next three you will have special powers over air. Had my sons lived they would have excelled in land, water and air.'

Turning to Sagar's wife, Bharadwaj said, 'You lived a false life with Sagar, even though he gave you pure love. For cheating on him like this, you will continuously beg for his help as a prisoner of war in your next birth. You will meet your husband,

and he will be the army chief and save you from the prison. You have the chance to break your own chakras of rebirth when you sincerely love your husband in the next birth.'

A new journey was about to begin for these two souls. The soul of Varsha would next be a prisoner of war, begging and pleading for support from the soul of Sagar. Where would this meeting take place? What sort of people would they be at their next outing?

The Indus Challenge: Janam Two

Sagar was reborn as Rudra in Janam Two in 330 BC. It was at this time that people of Bharat were looking inwards, while the Macedonians led by Alexander the Great aggressively explored outwards and wanted to conquer the world. The kingdoms of Bharat were also threatened. In the second avatar (Janam Two) of Rudra during the tumultuous times of Alexander and Chanakya, he offered stunning clues and left a trail that offered several clues and answered many mysteries in our rich history. Rudra, heading the nine unknown men (NUM) army decoded the secrets to save humanity from cataclysm and extinction.

Rudra fought against the treachery of the enemies from within and saved his Mauryan emperor and his kingdom from plunging into chaos once again.

Rudra, the man who protected his emperor and his sons, was killed by poisons mixed with sacred water at a temple. The same sacred water that killed him welcomed him at his birth in the next karmic outing, The Conquest of the East (Royal Crown Returns): Janam Three. The same water that had killed him made him extraordinarily proficient in the maritime wars that took place during his next karmic journey. Rudra has returned as a great naval commander as Surya during the dominating era of Cholas in AD 1000.

Would he be able to break the shackles of destiny and overcome the curse in his new avatar as Surya?

Prologue

Kaliyuga 4100 (AD 1000)

The domination of the Cholas started with the efforts of Emperor Raja Raja Chola, who established his kingdom and military from his capital city of Thanjavur (anglicized as Tanjore) in modern-day Tamil Nadu.

The enemies could not bear his onslaught, yet he could not complete one agenda, which forever eluded his success.

His grandfather had won the war against the Pandyas but could not declare it as a triumph, really. The Pandya king fled with the coveted royal crown, the mythical aaram and a precious garland of pearls, leaving everything in the custody of the Lankan king.

Raja Raja Chola tried to restore their pride by capturing these regal jewels from the Lankans. Yet again, he could win the war but could not finish it as an emphatic victory. This time, it was the Lankan king who managed to flee with the Pandya regal jewels. Ultimately, Raja Raja Chola had to leave this task for his son Rajendra Chola.

Surya in his third avatar during the challenging time of Raja Raja Chola and Rajendra Chola shows the unbreakable spirit of taking this massive task on himself. He braved severe circumstances and at the same time dared to dream big. Will he succeed?

PART I

The Birth in a Sacred Bath

1

AD 1000, Karthik month, Day 12, Midnight…

The Rameswaram jail was built by the Chola king in the southernmost tip of the Chola kingdom, where the three oceans joined. It was here in Rameswaram where an ancient temple of Lord Shiva was built by Lord Ram. According to mythology, Lord Ram embarked upon his Lankan trip from Rameswaram to save his wife Sita from the Lankan king Ravan, who had abducted her.

Rameswaram was not just a temple town. It was a port town where all the traders and naval ships went via the narrow sea between Rameswaram and Lanka (modern-day Sri Lanka). The town was always busy with traders from many countries and also the Chola navy. The hustle and bustle created by the traders, the navy and the pilgrims were the highlights of the town.

On the eastern corner of the town, away from all the hustle and bustle, there was a small man-made rocky island with no signs of civilization. The place was a little more than a desolate island occupied by the occasional swarm of birds.

The isolated location made it ideal for the exile of war criminals. Tall walls guarded the prison; even an ant could not escape those well-guarded cells.

In this prison, there were four blocks, Block 1 to 4: jailer's office, visitors' room, dining hall, kitchen and medical room. They were primitive and lacked privacy. The male and female cells were separate.

Block-4 housed the worst inmates. Five cells at the end of it were designated as 'The Hole', where badly behaved prisoners would be sent for periods for punishment, often brutally so.

A strict daily routine taught inmates to follow the prison rules and regulations.

Prisoners would be woken up at sunrise, given some porridge for breakfast, and one hour later, all the prisoners had to start their work.

Each prisoner would be assigned work by the jail supervisor. Work varied from gardening, stone breaking to other such manual labour. Lunch was at midday and dinner was served early. Two hours after sunset, everyone had to retire to their cells that were locked up by the jail supervisors.

The prisoners were given four rights, namely medical attention, shelter, food and clothing. Punishments for bad behaviour were harsh and one had to work really hard.

There were a few escape attempts in the past, most were caught, and a few were swallowed by crocodiles kept in the water around the prison walls.

The Rameswaram prison had about 1,500 prisoners. Many such prisons were located in different parts of the Chola kingdom ruled by the great Emperor Raja Raja Chola, whose fame spread across various kingdoms of Dakshin Bharat, and Lanka and Srivijaya (modern-day Indonesia) kingdoms beyond the oceans.

The prison was under the control of one jail supervisor who was assisted by two females and two male assistants.

The prison was supported by cooks and a medical

assistance group. Each prisoner had to wear a uniform with the emblem of the Chola's symbol—the tiger.

Rameswar was under the grip of heavy showers. Amidst the pouring rains—a sudden sound—a shriek in a silent night woke the inmates of the prison.

'Oh, aiyoh! I can't bear this pain any more. Oh! God, take this pain away from me.'

The prisoner Svarnamuki known as Svarna was yelling at the top of her voice. Her fellow inmates Kaveri and Poonkothai rushed towards her. They called the jailer Dheeran for help.

Dheeran knew that Svarna was pregnant and was going to deliver soon. Many a time, he tried to convince her to go to a hospital for delivery. Svarna (twenty-five) was a tough lady. She never listened to anyone. During her advanced pregnancy, she was surrounded by her co-inmates and two female jail assistants. The nurse on emergency duty was called in to attend to her.

'Aiyoh, aiyoh, the pain is unbearable. Do something nurse, take this goddamn baby out. Who asked for this baby? Please give me some water. I feel thirsty. I am going to die. Give me water, WATER!' Svarna said, shouting.

The nurse had taken sacred water as prasad from the Rameswaram temple that evening. She gave it to Svarna, asked her to drink it up, and told her to push the child out.

Svarna kept pushing after gulping down the sacred water.

'No, the pain is too much, do something nurse,' Svarna yelled.

The nurse immediately looked for other options—she planned for a water birth. Since the baby had been in the fluid sac for nine months, birthing in a similar environment was gentler for the baby and less stressful for the mother.

Svarna was taken to a tub filled with warm water for a water birth.

'Take a deep breath and push, Svarna,' the nurse kept telling her.

One last push—and there came out the head, and later the rest of the body of the baby. At last, after all the struggles, a baby boy was born in a water tub at the jail. The baby was quite messy and was covered with blood and vernix.

The nurse exclaimed, 'Ah, the sacred water enabled you to release the baby quickly. Let me wipe and wash him in the sacred water. He is born in the water. One day, he will rule the water, mark my words, Svarna...'

The nurse then cut the umbilical cord, and the baby was released from the mother, even though he could not be released from prison.

The nurse cleared the mucus around his body, wrapped him up in a blanket and gave the baby to Svarna for a cuddle.

However, an unexpected reaction came from her, which astonished everyone around!

2

'Don't bring that baby to me, I never wanted this goddamn child. I tried to kill it right at its embryonic stage.'

Svarna was too violent to control. Meanwhile, the baby had to be fed. The nurse looked at the boy. Unmindful of what was happening around him, he was smiling. His cute smile mesmerized the nurse.

Svarna was hysterical. She moved forward to grab her baby. The nurse thought, *She is in a state of mental disorder*.

Svarna shouted at her baby, 'Bastard, why are you born in this world? Your father ditched me and ran away as a traitor of the Chola kingdom. Not only that, he dragged me into this rotten jail of the Cholas. Are you born to follow in the footsteps of your father?'

Saying this, she snatched the baby and tried to kill him by dropping him on the floor.

'Jailer, Jailer. Please, get here,' the shrieking voice of the nurse shook Dheeran.

Dheeran ran in to save the baby and managed to do so. Looking at the baby, he said, 'Such impressive features this boy has.'

He noticed a big black birthmark on the baby boy's left chest which was in the shape of a fish.

'Surya,' he spontaneously called out. *This boy is special. The boy is going to rule the samudra* (sea), he thought.

'Surya, my Samudra Raja,' he fondly addressed the

newborn. The nurse chipped in.

'Jailer Dheeran, the baby has special features. He was born after I gave the Rameswaram temple's sacred water to his mother. Not only that, it was a water birth for him—his mother gave birth to him in the water. We also washed the boy with sacred water. Now, you pointed out he has a big fish-shaped birth mark on his chest. He will be recognized as the rising sun of the sea. Surya will be the perfect name.'

While the conversation was going on, Svarna was delirious. She kept on scolding the newborn. She refused to feed him.

But the baby had to be fed mother's milk. Dheeran was confused where to get it from.

3

Dheeran's mind started working in different directions. First, he should save the boy. Second, Svarna's hysterical behaviour had to be controlled.

He asked the attendants to take Svarna into her cell and lock her inside it. He also thought about bringing a female medical counsellor for counselling her.

Now, how to protect the boy, Surya? Suddenly, a thought crossed Dheeran's mind. His sister-in-law, Selvi, wife of his elder brother Vikraman, the southern region naval commander, had given birth to a boy just two days ago. Dheeran thought that he would request her to feed Surya along with her son.

Surya was fortunate to have the mother's milk from Dheeran's sister-in-law.

The boy was soon removed from the vicinity of his mother. Dheeran thought, *After a few days Svarna will be all right and she'll behave normally with her child.*

Meanwhile, a medical counsellor was arranged for Svarna. The medical counsellor tried to find out why Svarna hated her newborn.

Svarna started opening up. She recalled, 'Raja Raja Chola completely destroyed the Lankan kingdom and King Mahinda ran away to the south of Lanka. The Cholas confiscated their treasures. They transported them in different ships to the Chola kingdom.'

Raja Raja Chola asked one of his commanding officers,

Kumara Bahu, to oversee the safe dispatch of these treasures.

Kumara Bahu once met Svarna who was known as Svarnamuki, a beautiful courtesan who entertained the army personnel in the war camps with her mesmerizing dance. She claimed to have been born to a Lankan soldier and a Tamil courtesan in the war zone in Lanka.

Kumara Bahu and Svarna fell in love at first sight. She conceived before their marriage. They were both on one of the ships carrying the confiscated treasures to the Chola kingdom. They were about to get married at Rameswaram after the ship was to deliver the materials carried for the Chola kingdom. She never knew that the ship was carrying precious treasures back to the kingdom in that journey. She always thought that it was a specially arranged trip with her lover just before their wedding. But things turned ugly that night.

4

The betrothed—Kumara Bahu, Svarna—and a few crew members were there on the ship along with the treasures that were to be transported to Rameswaram.

While the ship was sailing from the north of Lanka towards Rameswaram, in the mid-sea, they were surrounded by the Lankan army men supported by Srivijaya and Chinese pirates.

They came into the ship and talked to Kumara Bahu. They tempted him with rulership of one of the eastern islands in exchange for the treasures.

Kumara Bahu initially refused the offer fearing for his life, as deserting Raja Raja Chola would be catastrophic. But he was lured by their offers of a small kingdom island in the far-east near Srivijaya. He kept talking to one of the pirates who was wearing a mask. He repeatedly talked to him about something. After hesitating for a while, something changed his mind. He might have thought going off to the far-east away from the Chola kingdom would enable him to move away from the vicinity of Raja Raja Chola. She confessed, 'Unfortunately he became a victim of his own greed. He who gives up his loyalty and bondage to the nation for an uncertain advantage, will not get anything in life.'

I do not know what got into him but in my opinion his greed destroyed his years of reputation, I thought I had wedded an unpatriotic person with no conviction in life. As some people would like to believe, even as a courtesan, we entertain the audience with our dance in order to remove their tiredness, but we never go to bed with different men. Our conviction to our marriage is deep, we never change our life partners. But I saw my life partner changing his loyalty within a fraction of time. I then decided to get away from him. I learned to hate all traitors and there is no disease that I spit on more than treachery. I refused his offer to go to the new far-eastern island kingdom of his. He deserted me and went with the pirates towards the far-eastern territories along with the Chinese pirates and, of course, with the treasures won by the Chola kingdom.

'When our ship was captured by the Chola navy near Rameswaram, I was in the ship all alone. None of my explanations could convince the navy. I became a prisoner here for no fault of mine.'

'My husband's fault and that traitor's greed pushed me into this prison. I want to erase the traitor from my mind. But alas, he left his imprint in the form of this boy.'

'I tried to erase this shameful leftover right at its embryonic stage. But my efforts were foiled. Now the traitor has come to haunt me in the form of this newborn. Let me destroy him! Let me destroy him!'

Svarna fainted with these words and the emergency medical team was called for further assistance.

5

Svarna opened her eyes after water was splashed on them. Several rounds of counselling happened where she was explained that the newborn should not be held responsible for the mistakes of his parents. Every time she gave a semblance of accepting this reality, but soon she would go back to the status quo of hating the child.

Dheeran tried to bring Surya every day to the prison and made Svarna see him. He was trying to create a bond between them. *The son may outgrow his mother's lap but never her heart*, he thought. There is no heaven that can be better than the heart of a loving mother.

'I don't believe in love at first sight because my mother started loving me even before she saw me. But why is Svarna defying the normal tendency of a pure mother's love for her child?'

Dheeran could not find any proper answer. However hard he tried to create a bond between Svarna and Surya, all his efforts failed. At times, Svarna tried to kill Surya, when she was asked to embrace him. *Forget the mother's milk, at least a warm embrace will happen*, Dheeran thought.

Surya was growing into a toddler, started muttering words, and captivated all the inmates of the prison other than his mother.

A big change occurred when he turned three.

PART II

The Adoption of the Orphan Surya

6

Karthika month, Day 12, Surya's third birthday...

There was a grand celebration at Vikraman's house.

Vikraman's wife had breastfed Surya along with her newborn son Maran. Svarna gave him up totally even though Dheeran tried to establish a bond between the mother and the son over the past three years.

During this period, Surya was growing up in the prison, and at Dheeran's and his brother's house. When Surya was growing this way, many of the inmates of the prison became friendly with him. Some of the nasty prisoners used to make fun of him—asking him about his father. Surya used to come back to Dheeran asking him about his father.

His mother refused to disclose the details of his father but for the sketchy references she made to her counsellor. She continued to boycott her son. Her animosity towards him never reduced. She did not even know he was named Surya. She never acknowledged the very existence of her son. She was living in her own world.

Dheeran could not see the boy suffering for no fault of his. The boy was branded a bastard. Dheeran thought as he would grow older, the society would ridicule him. With the intention of reaching out to Surya's father, Dheeran tried to elicit more information about him from Svarna but he could not get any lead.

Meanwhile, his brother Vikraman and Selvi were getting fond of Surya, even more than Maran. One day, Vikraman categorically announced that he would formally adopt Surya as his son when he turned three.

There was a function organized at Vikraman's house on the third birthday of Surya. Celebrations began in a grand way.

7

Datta homam

Datta homam was a ceremonial adoption. The ceremony was important to solemnize an adoption. Vikraman, being the southern naval commander, invited eminent men from the Chola army along with his friends and relatives.

Priests from the Rameswaram temple were performing the rituals. The rituals commenced with the Lakshmi Ganapati homam, a ritual believed to remove obstacles and bring prosperity, followed by 'Rudram' and 'Chamakam' both recitations from the Yajur Veda that praise Lord Shiva and finally datta homam, a ritual in which ghee and other offerings are given to the God through the medium of fire. The other offerings consisted of milk, curd, sugar, saffron, grains, coconut, perfumed water, incense, seeds, petals and herbs. These were ritually offered as a sacrifice to fire by way of religious propitiation.

There had to be a giving and taking ceremony. The boy comes out of his natural gotra to that of the adopted one.

The person receiving the boy was Vikraman, but who would put him up for adoption? Who would act as his father? Dheeran volunteered.

Vikraman then declared in front of the assembled guests, 'I, Vikraman along with my wife Selvi hereby solemnly declare that we adopt Surya as our son. He is no longer an orphan. From today he will be entitled to all the rights as our son and we undertake to bring him up as a responsible citizen. We hereby declare that we are the parents of Surya forever.'

All the guests applauded, congratulated the new parents and Surya. Dheeran's eyes were filled with tears. Surya was in safe hands now, and he wished the child a prosperous future.

What happened to Svarna then?

8

Svarna became normal once she forgot her son. She became quiet and peaceful.

She was let off from prison after serving a jail term of three years. After leaving the jail, she left the city. No one knew where she had gone. Dheeran tried to locate her by looking for her in nearby places. But all his efforts were in vain.

Eventually, he gave up since he thought Surya was safe with his adopted parents.

Slowly Svarna faded away from the memory of the people of the Rameswaram jail. Dheeran heard from some sources that she had become a Buddhist nun and renamed herself as Sister Nivedita.

PART III
The Beginning of Surya's Royal Connection

9

Surya was growing up in the house of Vikraman and Selvi as their son. One day, Vikraman noticed the birthmark of a big fish on the left chest of Surya. Dheeran mentioned to him that he is a special child.

Many a time when Vikraman took Surya and Maran to the Rameswaram seashore, where the three oceans merge. Surya showed a deep interest in swimming even at the age of four.

Vikraman, being a naval commander familiar with the sea, observed a few special qualities in him.

Surya was able to remain underwater for an extended period of time without breathing. He had the ability to haul great weights through water while swimming. He was sure-footed in wet and slippery areas.

He had the ability to communicate with large marine fishes and mammals with his touch, whisper and eye contact. He could listen well even when he was underwater.

He could create small eddies and whirlpools in the water. He could feel the tides and currents in open seas, rivers and bays. He could see clearly underwater, keep his eyes open for a long time without any harmful effects. He could even walk on water up to hundred yards at a stretch, predict the existence of moving animals or any underwater structures by keeping his ears above water, read the direction ships would sail to from a distance by looking at the movements of the sails and waves.

Was he a born marine warrior? Dheeran called him by his pet name Samudra Raja.

Is he a Samudra Raja? Vikraman would wonder.

He had all the characteristics of a great marine commander. Could he one day become the chief naval commander of the Chola kingdom then? Vikraman's thoughts were interjected by Selvi, 'Again you start dreaming about your son, Surya. He is only six years old, too young to think about his career. Relax please.'

'No, Selvi, he is a born marine commander. I am going to take him with me on naval ships during my voyages to Lanka, where our naval base is stationed now. Our emperor, Raja Raja Chola, captured the entire northern Lanka, destroyed Anuradhapura. Our big naval base is stationed at the Lankan ports. Our Crown Prince Rajendra frequently made surprise trips there to check the preparedness of our forces. I am going to take Surya with me there.'

'Are you mad? He is only six, do not joke with me. He is a child, not to be exposed to war fronts.'

'No, Selvi, he is born to achieve, he is going to rule the sea, my intuition says. I do not want to delay his karmic sea journey any more. You are protecting Maran. Surya is going to be my boy, he is going to achieve laurels at a young age. Do not stop me.'

The next day Surya was sea-bound along with his father. Surya's sea journey had commenced.

10

Surya's remarkable skill set identified by Vikraman at a very young age brought him to the sea.

During the sea voyage, stars sparkling in the sky, tidal waves of the sea, the fresh wind moving the ships, were all new experiences for Surya.

He was moving to all the levels of the ship—there were three levels. In a short time, he could get a grasp of the ship. A level focusing on moving the ship, one level ready with the long arrows to attack enemy ships, one level in the upper deck with open-air halls—it was an awe-inspiring experience for him.

He also went to the food section and saw a group preparing the meals. He became the darling of all the crew since having a child on a warship was unusual.

Vikraman always kept an eye on Surya, even though he allowed him to move freely inside the ship.

The warship was taking a full round of Lanka, calling at all the ports. At each port, Vikraman would spend a day and discuss with the local naval commanders about various issues around their preparedness.

Mahinda, the king of the Anuradhapura kingdom, after being defeated by Raja Raja Chola had fled to the southeastern part of Lanka known as Ruhuna. The Cholas ruled the northern part of Lanka renaming their capital Polonnaruwa as Jannantha Mangalam.

With Mahinda still controlling the southern part of Lanka, the Chola army was always in a state of alertness.

Surya spent almost three months in such an environment, and was about to return to Rameswaram to be with his mother and brother. At this time, a totally unexpected event happened.

11

One night the ship was calm on board. Surya's father was tense. He was waiting for a guest. The ship was about to start from the Lankan port for their voyage towards Rameswaram.

The guest his father was expecting was probably a higher authority, which is why he was tense. One of the cabin rooms on board the ship was getting a quick facelift. Who could the guest be?

Within a short while, the answer was there. A royal family member with his bodyguards entered the ship to a grand welcome from Vikraman.

He was talking to the guest in a husky voice. Was he a royal family member on a secret journey? The warship took its voyage under the captaincy of Surya's father. It was midnight. Suddenly, the sounds around them forced Surya to wake up. He realized his father was talking to the royal guest who came in before the ship moved from the shore.

'Your Majesty, you take risks. You come for surprise checks, your presence lifts the positive attitude of our armed forces who stay away from their families for years. But you are our crown prince who cannot afford to take such risks on the war front.

'Now we are surrounded by enemy warships. Somehow, your presence here, a well-guarded secret has reached the enemy camp. We are not prepared for a war, as Your Majesty's visit was a surprise one, not known to anyone even in our Chola kingdom. Everyone is under the impression that you are in our capital city Thanjavur. What can we now do? I cannot afford to allow anything happening to you under my captaincy, Your Majesty.'

Vikraman's voice was shaking. Surya could guess that there was a crisis. He also understood that the royal guest was none other than Crown Prince Rajendra Chola, the greatest warrior prince. The crown prince had come on a secret mission, but was now surrounded by his enemies. This he could understand. *Where do we go from here?* he asked himself.

12

When Vikraman was in his worst crisis-like situation the crown prince was in his best mood. He was somehow not at all bothered by this crisis.

'Vikraman, a calm sea never produces a skillful mariner. No pain, no gain, why are you worried? Navigating on the shores on shallow water will not lead you to new discoveries. Taking a risk is my way of life. Instead of discussing my appetite for risk, we should now focus on how to get out of this crisis.

'Tell me, how many of our army men are here including my bodyguards? I understand we are also transporting some of our army forces in this ship back to our kingdom from the Lankan war zone.'

'Your Majesty, we have about one hundred army men on board the ship. But none of them knows you are here. What can we do then? The Lankan forces surrounding us are in their four ships in all the directions. Each has a minimum of five hundred soldiers—both navy and army. They outnumber us in terms of weapon and men strength.'

'Calm down, Vikraman, we will chalk out our strategy. I saw your boy travelling with you. Leave him with me for now. I will change into a different attire.

'I will mix with the crowd of our own soldiers. I become an ordinary soldier among them. Allow the opponents to get inside our ship. Do not fight. Give the impression that we've surrendered.

'Once we surrender, let them identify me among the soldiers. None of them recognize me by my face. As a matter of fact, even many of our soldiers do not recognize me.

'While they carry out the identity parade, from all directions of the ship, one soldier will jump into the sea with a small boat. I will be one of them. The enemy will not know which one has the crown prince.

'Send your boy with me. Rest I will take care.'

'Your Majesty, how will my boy who is just six years old be able to help you? I am confused'.

'Vikraman, we have no time, do what I said, surrender now. I am joining the soldiers in the guise of a Lankan fisherman along with your son. Remember, I am one of the five Lankan fishermen captured by you, and chained by you. Let the other four prisoner fishermen get ready on board. All five of them will be chained and kept as prisoners in a corner. Be quick, execute the plan. Go, surrender. The operation begins now.'

Vikraman had no other option. He raised a white flag, a signal of surrender. Given the sensitivity involved, he was not afraid of the enemy but was afraid of the outcome. His fear came true, as he encountered his enemy.

13

The enemy camp was led by Jayanthan, the cruel commander of the Lankan forces. He was the one who led the escape of Mahinda from Anuradhapura.

He was waiting for a tit-for-tat situation and it was now that he had got the opportunity.

Jayanthan entered the Chola ship led by Vikraman. He was accompanied by about a hundred of his commandos.

'Are you the captain of this ship? What is your name? Where is your tiger, your crown prince? Today we catch the big fish. He destroyed our forces with his father a few years ago. Today we will teach a great lesson to your kingdom. Tomorrow morning your emperor Raja Raja Chola will kneel in front of us begging for the release of his brave warrior son—Rajendra Chola. We never expected that your crown prince will come to our territory and get trapped so soon. It is a great day for us, Captain. What is your name, again?'

'Vikraman is my name. What do you need from us? We have surrendered to you. We obey your command now. Who told you our crown prince is here? Why would he navigate into this warship? He is a crown prince of the greatest kingdom. You might have been given the wrong information.'

'You are clever, Vikraman. We will enforce an identification parade. Ask all your people to assemble at the third-level upper deck,' commanded Jayanthan.

The identification parade was arranged. The Lankans

started the inspection.

They could not identify Rajendra Chola. The Lankans did not miss upon seeing the fishermen prisoners.

'Anyway, no one is identifying your Crown Prince Rajendra Chola. We know he is amongst you. That is no worry for us. We will put you all in our jail, once we take you to our kingdom. If your crown prince is not identified, let him, stay in our prison. What do we lose?' Jayanthan shouted.

Oh, no, if they were all imprisoned in their jails, what will happen to Rajendra Chola? thought Vikraman. But strange things happened next.

14

It was midnight: an Amavasya day. Jayanthan and his Lankan soldiers completed their identification parade and started chaining the Chola soldiers and naval men.

At this stage, from all the four corners of the ship, they heard a few people jumping into the sea. Jayanthan soon realized that some of them had tried to escape.

He announced, 'All of you, note this. If you jump into the sea, our patrolling ships will kill you. If you remain in the ship at least you can save your life.'

He then expedited the process of chaining the Chola soldiers and started moving them to the lower deck. He ordered his guards to catch the ones who had escaped.

He waved red flags to his other ships surrounding them, alerting them about the enemies who had escaped.

Rajendra Chola smartly arranged the escape of soldiers into four directions of the ship at the same time, as that would complicate the search process of the Lankan enemy camp. Using this time, he thought he would escape.

He was one among those who jumped out. His idea of taking Surya along with him was to add credibility to his story that he was a fisherman who had lost his way and reached mid-sea. His son was also with him. He was struggling to get back to the shore. The presence of a boy with him would add more credibility to his version. Since he can speak the Sinhalese language, his explanation would get him out of any

Lankan interceptor. That is why he was so confident when he was talking to Commander Vikraman.

His calculations were spot-on. The presence of Surya, the fisherman get-up of Rajendra Chola and his fluent Sinhalese saved them from being caught.

He had brought Surya for a limited purpose, but that boy did wonders that completely surprised the crown prince.

15

Even though they came out unscathed from one of the interceptors, they were not yet out of danger. Too many patrolling boats were in the vicinity. It appeared one of them caught hold of one of the escapees from the ship. Hence the search was at its best.

When the crown prince was worried, Surya did something exceptional. He placed his hands into the water from the boat and mixed the water with both his hands. He could create ripples first which later became small eddies and whirlpools. He asked the crown prince to row the boat in all four directions for a while, and he kept creating those whirlpools. The crown prince saw one of the patrolling boats getting caught in that whirlpool and capsizing into the sea. *What a brilliant skill set this boy has!* the crown price thought.

These whirlpools became defence walls in the sea for the boat of the crown prince. The patrolling boats could not cross the lines of whirlpools, which were artificially created by Surya.

Having denied access to the Lankan patrolling boats, the next challenge was to reach the Chola zone of the sea, away from the visibility of the Lankan zone and also to reach the shore from mid-sea. It was totally dark. *How do we reach the destination?* This was the next question on the mind of the crown prince. He was worried since he did not know the extraordinary skill set of Surya.

However, Surya was oblivious to the worries of the crown

prince. He was doing something else. He jumped into the sea. He kept his ears close to the water, dipped his hand into it and felt the direction of the movement of the waves. *What was he doing?* the crown prince thought.

He saw Surya walking a few steps on the water. Then Surya came back into the boat. He told the crown prince that the wind was blowing in the northern direction and within a short distance in the north, there were ship movements. As they were in the Chola zone, there was a high probability that the ships could be Chola navy ships.

'Once we reach the ships in the Chola-controlled waters, we can reach Rameswar', he said.

The crown prince could not believe that he would be guided by a six-year-old boy. He was in awe of Surya.

As it was Amavasya, the tidal waves were strong. The small boat was struggling mid-sea. Surya, the wonder boy, had a solution. He jumped into the sea, started swimming and at the same time started hauling the boat through the water towards the northern direction. *Unbelievable, it is too good to believe*, the crown prince thought.

After a while they could sight of a ship, a flag flying on top of it had the emblem of the Chola kingdom—the tiger.

But without any flag or any other instrument, how could we show signals to the ship, the crown prince thought. Surya had a solution for that as well. He took the raja mudra (the official seal of the Chola kingdom) in the form of a ring from the prince and started walking on the water towards the ship.

16

Surya took the rope hanging out of the ship, went inside and alerted the ship captain, who refused to believe that their Crown Prince Rajendra Chola was in distress in mid-sea.

Then he showed the the raja mudra of the crown prince. Immediately, they took steps to receive their crown prince.

The ship captain was strictly instructed not to divulge this information to anyone, as it will be kept as a 'Rajanga Secret', a secret so powerful that it is required to be protected at all cost. The public or the enemy should never know that the Chola crown prince was ever in distress.

When the ship reached Rameswaram, Surya left with his family. The crown prince left for Thanjavur using his camouflaged identity.

A few days later, Vikaraman returned to his house at Rameswaram and Surya told him what had happened. Vikraman was a proud father. But he could not share this with all his friends and relatives as this episode had to be kept as a closely guarded secret.

But Surya was interested to know how Vikraman returned from the enemy ship. He said that the crown prince on his return sent seven warships with more than 2,000 army men to mid-sea. They destroyed the Lankan ships and brought back all the Chola soldiers along with Vikraman and his ship.

'But for the quick action of our crown prince, we would be jailed in the prison of Mahinda,' said Vikraman.

When Vikraman and Selvi were rejoicing over the achievements of Surya, an unexpected development took place.

PART IV

Surya: The Royal Navy Commander

17

Chola Royal Army School, Thanjavur

Surya was dropped at the Chola Royal Army School by his father.

'Such a young boy, what will he do in a hostel so far away?' his mother said with despair.

'No worries, Selvi, this school adopts children from the age of six. They graduate at the age of sixteen. All aspects of the Chola Army are taught to them. They are assigned a "guru", a reputed warrior who does not go to battlefields after the age of fifty. Each guru is assigned six students so that their focus is not diluted,' Vikaraman explained.

'Our son Maran could not get the opportunity to study at this Royal Army School, as it is meant for royal family children and boys with special skills, identified by various methods. These boys are groomed for our Chola military leadership. Surya is lucky to have got this opportunity.'

But Selvi was unconvinced.

'Maybe as a mother, I do not see my child as an adult worker at this tender age. I only look at his well-being as a child. A mother's love is not logical,' Selvi said.

'Do not worry, Surya has been assigned Guru Bramendra, he is one of the finest warriors. He won many wars for our kingdom. He will take good care of Surya.'

It was time for them to hand over Surya to Guru Bramendra.

'Welcome Vikraman, where are you posted now? Last time when we met was during the Lankan War, you told me you are in the Chola navy, southern division,' Guru Bramendra said.

'Yes, Guruji, now I am the southern regional naval commander, posted at Rameswaram. My son Surya is fortunate enough to get admission here under your tutelage.'

'I have heard of your son Surya. At a very young age, he did something rather commendable by saving our Crown Prince Rajendra under dramatic circumstances. I came to know that he has some extraordinary skills in water. He is a "Samudra Raja", our crown prince has written his recommendation, so you leave him with me and go back to your place without any worry. He is my boy from today.'

The parents reluctantly bid goodbye to their son.

18

Bramendra, Amuda Vendan, Miladuyar, Kandamaran and Veera Sena were the retired warriors of Raja Raja Chola who were assigned six boys each. A total of thirty boys were taken in for the batch under the 'direct military leadership programme'.

Each of these warriors would bring up these boys under his tutelage. They would be formally trained in the school together, but they would be staying with their assigned gurus, in their quarters.

On the very first day at school, Surya met his mates. The other five boys in his gurukul included:

- Arul Mozhi (defence minister Krishna Raman's son);
- Vetri (spy force chief's son);
- Selvan (weapon force chief's son);
- Manukesary (Rajendra Chola's seventh son, later conferred the title Sundara Keralan); and
- Li Yuang, a Chinese boy.

How come a boy who looks completely different from us is here in this school? Surya thought.

He got his answer soon.

Guru Bramendra introduced each one of them. Many of them were from royal families. But Surya and Li Yuang were the only non-royal family members, who joined on the basis of their special skills.

'My dear boys, welcome to my gurukul. From today, you

will always be with me. I will take you to the Royal Army School every day and you will stay with me at my house. Treat me like your father and my wife Savitri will be your mother.'

'Now let me introduce you to this boy from Chinese culture. Li Yuang's father was a pirate. His name was Naboodha and he belonged to the Mongolian tribe. He married a Chinese woman and their child is Li Yuang.'

'While our Emperor Raja Raja Chola was on his expedition to Lanka, he encountered pirates led by Naboodha. Our emperor overpowered their ship and when Naboodha was about to die, he handed over Li Yuang to our emperor saying, "Emperor, please educate my son and make him your naval commander one day. He lost his mother, now he is going to lose his father. Let piracy go away along with my generation. Let him lead a life where he doesn't have to be a pirate. Please promise me, you will make him a sea commander one day."'

'Our emperor was moved and brought Li Yuang here to our country and admitted him to this school.'

Each of them looked at each other, smiled at one another and got friendly. New friendships were blossoming…

19

The next day, lessons started in the class of thirty students with six gurus.

Bramendra started addressing the class, 'Boys, do you all know the rich history of the Cholas? Our emperors have achieved great things in their lives. Let me tell you about our rulers' rich history now.'

The boys eagerly listened to their rulers' history.

'The Chola race, the solar race, starts with Manu Neethi Chola or the one who upholds justice at all times. When a calf was mistakenly killed by a chariot driven by the king's own son, the mother cow sought justice by ringing the justice bell, which was kept for the public by the king. He went on to serve justice favouring the mother cow, even though it was against his son.

'For saving a dove from an eagle, King Sibi volunteered to give flesh from himself. From this Chola race came Karaikal Chola, who built the first dam on the Cauvery River. So many famous kings such as Nalankilli, Nedungkilli, Killi Valavan came from this race. Boys, are you all listening?

'All these kings built temples and gave excellent governance, ruling the Chola kingdom from Kaveri Poompattinam (Poombuhar). They even operated the navy from their capital.

'Like the sun sets and rises again, the time shadowed the Chola race for a while, yet again the light came with Vijayalaya around Kaliyuga 3950 (AD 850) about 150 years ago.

'Now we are in Kaliyuga 4107 (AD 1007).

'Vijayalaya stood with the Pallavas against their war with the Pandyas. The Thirupurambiyam battle sealed the victory over the Pandyas. He took ninety-six injuries on his body, displaying his bravery. He established his capital at Thanjavur with a great temple for Nishumbhasudini, the goddess of shakti. It was the foundation of our current Chola kingdom.

'Then came King Aaditya, who caused the demise of the Pallavas, defeated the Pandys and expanded the Chola kingdom. He was followed by his son Parantaka, who conquered parts of Lanka and also defeated the expanding Rashtrakuta dynasty.

'The king and princes of our Chola kingdoms took to the battlefield themselves. They never shied away from direct participation in a battlefield. Boys, you too should be brave enough to take the battles head-on. Never shy away from direct participation on the battleground. Learn about this from Crown Prince Rajaditya, the heir apparent to King Parantaka.

'The heroic Rajaditya, ornament of the solar race, having shaken the unshakable Rashtrakutas with his forces, was himself pierced in his heart while seated on the back of a large elephant by the sharp arrows of the enemy. He earned the praise of the three worlds and ascended to the heaven of heroes.

'Any questions now, boys?' The guru stopped.

Surya chipped in, 'Guruji, couldn't the prince be saved by his soldiers?'

'My dear boy, this is leading from the front. Unless a leader fights a battle from the front, the soldiers may not be motivated enough.

'When you battle from the front, uncertainty is the certainty. Anything can appear. Loyalty and devotion lead to bravery. Bravery leads to the spirit of self-sacrifice. The spirit of self-sacrifice creates trust. Bravery creates leaders.

'Be brave, my boys, battle it out by taking it head-on, do not shy away. Let us meet tomorrow. Now the class ends for the day.'

The boys dispersed.

20

The boys went home thinking about Rajaditya, the crown prince who gave up his life fighting at the battlefield. They felt goosebumps.

The next day...

The boys were eagerly waiting for the lecture on Chola history.

'Since Rajaditya died in the war during his lifetime, King Parantaka's second son Gandaraditya came to power. He was detached from the worldly matters and had spiritual interests. He did not want to pursue wars.

'Soon Gandaraditya's brother Arinjaya followed him for a short while. This was a time when the Chola empire was shadowed by clouds. Since Gandaraditya's son Uthama Chola was a child, even though he had the rights to the throne, it was Arinjaya's son Sundara Chola who became the ruler.

'Sundara Chola won wars against the Pandyas. His son, Crown Prince Aditya Karikala, was killed under suspicious circumstances.

'After Sundara Chola, his brother Uthama Chola who had the rights to the throne came to power. But Sundara Chola's son and our present ruler Raja Raja Chola was widely preferred by the public. But Raja Raja Chola gave way for his uncle Uthama Chola to avoid civil war in the country. For sixteen long years, Raja Raja Chola widely travelled across the kingdom and established people to people contact. Who killed his brother Crown Prince Aditya Karikala? The question was always in his mind.

'He found out that the tantric Brahmins of the same Chera kingdom (maderu-day Kerala) who were once ministers to his uncle Uthama Chola, were the key culprits. Raja Raja Chola asked Uthama Chola to leave the post of the king, which Uthama Chola agreed to do without dissent.

'Raja Raja Chola became a ruler in his middle age after waiting for sixteen long years. He came to power in the Kaliyuga year 4085 (AD 985).

'Once in power, Raja Raja Chola fought many wars. All the enemies—Pandiyas, Chalukyas, Rashtrakuta and Pallavas were defeated. He also crossed the ocean to Lanka and won the northern part of Lanka.

'The tantric Brahmins of the Chera kingdom—Ravi Dasa, Parameswara and Soman—who were instrumental in killing Crown Prince Aditya Karikala were driven away from the Chola kingdom with their families.

'Later when these people still tried to show their resistance to our Chola kingdom from the army training school of Kandalur, Raja Raja Chola broke their back and all of them ran away to other countries. Their whereabouts are still not known to us.

'Our ruler Raja Raja Chola has a great personality—his excellent character and competence singles him out from the rest.'

The classes for the day ended. The boys were longing to know more about their current ruler Raja Raja Chola.

21

'Do you want to know more about Raja Raja Chola, my dear boys? Guruji asked the students.

'Yes, Guruji, we have been waiting to hear more about him since yesterday,' the boys shouted together.

'During the Chalukya war, the river Tungabhadra was overflowing. The Chola army was wondering how to cross it. While the army was thinking, our ruler swam across the river with his horse. He was the first person to reach the opposite bank of the river, not only that he killed forty opponent soldiers with his sword and thundered—"Are there any more to fight?" The opposite forces were totally shattered. Such is the courage of our ruler, do you understand, my boys?' asked Guruji.

'With the accession of our ruler, we enter upon a century of grandeur and glory for the dynasty of the Cholas. In the organization of the Civil Service and the army, in art and architecture, in religion and literature, we have excelled far beyond our contemporaries. From a relatively small state on his accession, from the disasters of the Rashtrakuta invasion, he has now established this kingdom into an extensive well-knit empire, efficiently organized and administered, rich in resources with a powerful standing army.

'Our current ruler's able governance attests his true personality and the firm grasp of his intellect allows nothing to escape his vigilance. The affection he is lavishing on his sister and the privileged position he has accorded to his grandaunt, the mother of King Uthama Chola, all indicate that he is a great noble man as well as a far-sighted ruler.

'A well-structured naval force has been created by our ruler which will take us to great heights in the future.

'Also, you should note this. Raja Raja Chola is a great statesman and a tolerant person. Even though an ardent follower of Lord Shiva, he constructed some temples for Lord Vishnu. He even encouraged the erection of the Chudamani Vihara in Nagapattinam by the Silendra King Vijaya Maravijayattungavarman. This vihara is dedicated to Lord Buddha. Nagapattinam is the first port of call touched by the vessels from the fareast.

'In order to enable the traders from the fareast to worship their god, our ruler permitted the erection of a vihara in this port town. Such was his religious tolerance.

'Now our ruler is constructing the great Brihadishvara temple in this capital city.

'Do you want to see our ruler Raja Raja Chola, my dear boys?'

'Yes, of course, Guruji,' the boys said unanimously.

'I promise, one of these days, I will take all of you to the temple under construction. That is where he spends most of his time these days.'

The boys went home excited about their meeting with the great ruler.

22

The next few months went off well for the boys. The six boys in the ward of Guru Bramendra were bonding. Surya and Li Yuang became thick friends. Nobody could understand how this bond between two boys from different races got established.

Friendship has no caste, creed or colour, Guruji thought.

One day, an interesting session started during the classes. It was about 'what triggers wars from the side of Cholas'. This question was raised by Surya.

He asked, 'Why do we invade other countries or for that matter why do we invade on our own at all?'

'Very interesting question at such a young age, my dear boy,' said Guruji.

The theme of the day focused on this subject.

'Why should a ruler wage a war? Boys note this: every country may have different reasons for waging a war than ours. For our Chola kingdom, the triggers for war are based on these reasons:

- We do not wage a war to amass wealth. We wage war to retain our supremacy.
- We wage a war when others invade us or cause problems for our countrymen: be it traders, peasants or ordinary citizens.
- We wage a war when our reputation is at stake.

- We wage a war when our allies request us to come to their rescue. Our war is based on raj dharma, we do not invade to loot.'

Having said that, I am going to tell you about an unfinished agenda of our rulers.'

'Unfinished agenda? How come we could not achieve this till date with all our might?' asked Arul Mozhi.

Then came the key historic event from the past of the Chola history, which led to the answer.

23

'About fifty years ago, our ruler Parantaka, our present ruler's great-grandfather, paved the way for the annexation of the Pandya kingdom, which had been troubling us for long.

'Frustrated in all his attempts to stem the tide of the Chola invasion, the Pandya King Raja Simha took to flight.

'The Pandya to diffuse the heat, quickly embarked for Lanka abandoning his kingdom inherited from his ancestors. He left his diadem, the mythical aaram and a precious garland of valuable pearls with a Lankan king for safe custody and then took shelter in the Chera kingdom.

'Parantaka wanted to celebrate his success by a formal coronation at the capital of the Pandya kingdom Madurai by investing himself with the insignia of the Pandya monarchy. So Parantaka chased them down in Lanka. However, the crown and the regal jewels could not be captured by our ruler.

'What is the meaning of the word 'insignia'? Can anyone tell me?' Guruji asked and then paused for a while. Observing their silence, he himself answered, 'Insignia is a distinguishing mark or sign of something. Here it is a distinguishing symbol of the Pandya kingdom, please understand this boys.'

Surya interjected, 'What is this mythical aaram?'

'Various poets have praised the garland in the past. They wrote: "On the breast of the Pandya king can be seen a garland painted with sandalwood paste, a string of pearls and a glittering jewelled garland of the king of gods. Long lives he who wears Lord Indra's garland on his chest".

'What is this mythical aaram of gods worn by Pandya kings? Here is the legend of the Indra aaram. Here is the legend, my dear boys…

'The ancient Pandya King Malayattuvchan and his wife Kanchani didn't have any child. So they performed a sacrifice and a daughter appeared in the sacrificial fire, an incarnation of Goddess Durga, aged three and with three breasts. They named her Tatakai and she ruled the kingdom. While trying to fight Lord Shiva in Kailasha, she fell in love with him and her third breast disappeared. She married Lord Shiva. Tatakai was from then on known as Meenakshi and Lord Shiva was known as Sundareswara.

'Ukkirapandya was born to the divine couple. Ukkirapandya (incarnate of Lord Muruga) was groomed to be the king and was married to Princess Kantimati (an incarnate of Valli, wife of Lord Muruga).

'After the marriage, Sundereswara told his son Indra that Varuna and Mount Meru were his enemies. I give you three weapons: a discus to aim at Lord Indra, a javelin to quell the sea and a club to strike Mount Meru down. Use them well.'

'During the reign of Ukkirapandya there was a great drought, followed by famine and misery. The Chola, Chera and Pandya kings went to see Lord Indra on the advice of Sage Agastya who predicted twelve years of drought. The kings went to Lord Indra to beg him to release the rain clouds.

'The Chera and Chola kings accepted the low and humble seats Lord Indra offered them. But Ukkirapandya went and sat on the same level as Lord Indra. The Chola and Chera kings offered precious gifts to Lord Indra and begged for rain, which Lord Indra granted. Ukkirapandya stood next to Lord Indra and looked as majestic as Lord Indra himself. Ukkirapandya's refusal to beg for rain made Lord Indra plot against him. So Lord Indra gave him an aaram to make him feel honoured.

'Under the pretext of honouring Ukkirapandya, Lord Indra presented him with an aaram. This aaram had reduced the strength of the mountain-like shoulders of many men. But Ukkirapandya accepted it and wore it swiftly on the neck. Nothing happened to him.

'The King of gods who had his kingdom in the sky saw this and was amused. He looked at Ukkripandya's chest which was adorned with a flower garland and bees were buzzing around it. He felt that from now on the world with refer to him as the Pandyan who sported the aaram of bees.

'To humiliate Ukkirapandya even more, Lord Indra didn't grant his land any rain. The Pandya king went to Podigaimalai and captured and imprisoned the large rain clouds that were especially dear to Lord Indra.

'Indra in a fury mounted his elephant and waged a war on Madurai. The Pandya attacked Lord Indra with his discus and broke his crown. Lord Indra's army was also crushed. Ukkirapandya then ordered Lord Indra to send rains in exchange for the clouds.

'The Indra aaram studded with glittering jewels lay decorated on the chest of Ukkirapandya and his lineage forever.'

The boys were spellbound...

'Did our ruler Raja Raja Chola not try to recapture the crown and royal jewels, Guruji?' one of the boys asked.

The boys were curious.

'Yes, Raja Raja Chola conquered northern Lanka. But King Mahinda again moved to the south of Lanka to the inaccessible hilly terrain of Rohana. Raja Raja Chola also could not succeed in capturing the crown and regal jewels from Rohana.

'The capture of the diadem, mythical aaram and the precious pearl garland of Pandya kingdom deposited with the Lankan kingdom continues to be an unfinished agenda.

'Maybe when our Crown Prince Rajendra Chola becomes our ruler, we may retrieve our pride. The Lankans hold it as custodians and not as conquerors. We have conquered the Pandyas and therefore we are the rightful owner of these regal jewels.

'Will you all join hands with our crown prince when you become our military leaders?

'I hope Lord Shiva will give me a long life to witness the grand occasion of our ruler wearing the crown and the glittering jewels won by us.'

That day, the class ended with hope.

24

The next few months of theory sessions involved lessons on the army, the navy, the ships, the types of weapons the Cholas use during the wars; the methods of recruitment in the army and military support services and the weapon-making units of the kingdom.

Among all these subjects, it was the Chola navy that interested Surya and Li Yuang the most, which made them take Chola navy as their elective subject.

The syllabus was taught by Naval Commander Bheema Sena. Some aspects of it were summarized for Li Yuang by Surya for their exams.

This is how he narrated:

'The Chola admirals commanded much respect and prestige in society. The naval commanders also acted as diplomats in some instances.

'The ruler Raja Raja Chola commissioned various foreigners—Arabs and Chinese in the naval-building programme.

'Many technological innovations from the Song dynasty of China were adopted in Chola ship designs. These were watertight compartments in the hull of the ship, the mariner's compass and many others.

'The Chola navy could undertake—combat, non-combat missions, peacetime patrol and interdiction of piracy; escort trade vessels; conduct naval battles close to home ports and at high seas; reinforce the army in times of need; sabotage the enemy vessels and so on.

'There were numerous sub-units from a Kanni which were no more than five vessels which were used for wartime special-purpose tactical formations to the grand Pirivu, a fleet of 1,000 ships headed by the king and confidant of the king.

'Supreme Commander is chakravarthy, the emperor.

'Commander-in-chief of the navy is jalathipathy, the admiral of the navy.

'Commander of the fleet is devar or nayagan (admiral).

'Fleet squadron commander is ganathipathy (rear admiral).

'Commander of the group is mandalithipathy (vice admiral).

'Commander of the ship is kalapathy (captain).

'Officer—arms in ship is kappu (executive officer—weapons).

'Officer—masts is seevai (master's chief and engineering officer).

'Officer—boarding party is eeitimaar (major/captain).

'Also, there were different cadres for auxiliary forces, customs and excise (sunga illaka), coast guards, privator navy's (trade guilds). Various naval weapons used are fire arrows, thermal weapons, spears, bows and arrows, javelin and so on.'

This will prepare Surya and Li Yuang with their elective subject too. Surya emerged as the topper in all the navy subjects. Guruji too called him 'Samudra Raja'.

25

The Chola army conferred graduation at the age of sixteen. Every year the graduation function was celebrated in a grand manner.

The crown prince presided over the military graduation every year. On this occasion, different regional commanders-in-chief and their officers selected recruits for their regions.

A full day of festivity was usually on. There were war games, debates and quiz programmes.

The quiz programmes were open for all the students from the entry level to the graduate level. There were three separate sections—one for cavalry, one for navy and for elephant forces.

Guruji Brahmendra nominated both Surya and Li Yuang for the navy force quiz. It was their first experience, they were both curious and anxious. There were fifteen participants from the ages of 6 to 16.

Surya was marvellous in his performance. He came out as the darling of the crowd. The answers given by Surya on the navy quiz were simply mind-blowing.

Q: *What is a magnetic compass? How is it used on sea?*
A: The needle of the compass will only be in the direction of the north. Based on this, the other directions can be identified. Wherever we turn, the compass needle will show the north direction. Thus sea directions can be identified with the compass.

Q: *What is a fire arrow?*
A: It is a short spear with a sharp edge. We Cholas cover the spearhead/arrows with cloth which is dipped in camphor oil. When it is lit and thrown, it creates the same effect as that of a Chinese fire arrow. The outcome is same, but the method is different.

Q: *What are the various forms of fire arrows used by our contemporaries?*
A: There are various forms of fire arrows used by different places in the past.

- Lit torches (burning sticks) were the earliest form of incendiary device is used. They were followed by incendiary arrows. The simplest flaming arrows had an oil-or resin-soaked tows tied below the arrowhead and were effective against wooden structures.
- The Chinese Song dynasty, our contemporary in China, created fire arrows—rockets attached to arrows and launched in mass through platforms. Mongols used primitive rockets made from bamboos and leather.

Q: *What are thermal weapons?*
A: Early thermal weapons used in warfare used heat to destroy or damage enemy personnel, fortifications or territories. The boiling water and hot sand could be poured on attacking personnel. Oil, resin, animal fat, hot pitch and similar compounds were used, substances such as quick lime could be toxic and blinding. Oil used to be sprayed on the decks of the ship, then ignited by shooting down flaming arrows.

Q: *How do we defend a thermal attack?*
A: Defence from thermal weapons and fire attacks were usually

water or other liquids such as urine. Hides were soaked and draped over vulnerable wooden hoardings and siege engines on a ship and barrels of water were collected and stored. Hides had to be hung in an overlapping manner so that water could run down the whole structure to extinguish flames.

Q: *What are the arms used by our Chola army and navy?*
A: Most standard weapons are used by both the army and the navy.

- Swords (val): Both curved and uncurved swords are used along with shields.
- Small sword (kuthuval): Thrusting weapon for close-range kills. This weapon is similar to a katar.
- Bow and arrow: Most standard composite bow is of bamboo material, measuring three to four hand-lengths with string made of bamboo fibre or other tough materials. Arrows with different material alloys ranging from copper alloys to different types of steels are used.
- Spear (eethi): General spear is made of iron alloy and the body consists of bamboo. A javelin is used occasionally.
- Battle axe (kodali/parasu): A special weapon used by cavaliers and infantry in some occasions.
- Boomerang (valari): Special weapon used by experts. This weapon is used to attack moving mid-ranged targets.
- The Chola navy has a flame-thrower which was incorporated by the Cholas supposedly following the Song dynasty.

Q: *How do we use the nature for navigation sea on?*
A: We should understand the change of direction of wind on our shoulders, sometimes on our lower backbone. We can see the direction through the movement of threads/robes. The currents can be seen by specially skilled eyes. The blue colour of currents will be different from the sea blue. The movement of fishes in a current will be different. Waves of tortoises will sail in water currents.

We should catch the current for sailing but must avoid it for anchoring. Based on the location of stars in the night we can predict directions and map known currents.

Q: *How is a good ship built?*
A: A ship is not made out of one type of wood. Neem, teak, pungai tree trunks are used based on the functionality of the parts, requirements of strength, elasticity, weightlessness and so on. The ropes are from palm tree fibres dipped in drumstick resin.

The answers were too good. Surya became the cynosure of everyone in the convocation hall. Obviously, he won the first prize at the quiz competition.

Rajendra Chola made a special mention about Surya. He said, 'I saw Surya once under dramatic circumstances in the sea as a young boy—younger than today's Surya. He is a child prodigy, and can create wonders on water. I want to see him one day as our jalathipaty (admiral of the Chola navy). God bless him.'

The crowd clapped. Surya's parents were proud of him.

Samudra Raja Surya was growing from strength to strength at his school.

26

After nearly five years of study at the Chola Army School, Surya learnt many aspects of the war. He was taking special interest in the navy.

One day, there was a special guest lecture by Krishna Raman, the defence minister of Raja Raja Chola, an erstwhile warrior, even though he hailed from a family of pandits. His son Arul Mozhi was Surya's classmate.

The boys had heard a lot about Krishna Raman, his war tactics and strategic brain. They listened to him attentively. He gave a special lecture on the Chola's spy network system.

'Boys, it is a great honour to address the budding Chola military leaders of tomorrow. Today, I will give you some interesting tips on our spy networks. A spy has to mix with our opponents, should observe what is happening in the opponent country and then pass the information on to his own country. This is a dangerous job. For developing spying skills, we have a special college in Thanjavur.

'We educate them on using swords, spears, javelin; boxing; climbing on walls at great heights; using ropes to climb up and down; chirping like birds and several other skills.

'We teach them how to flow with the river, stay underwater, use udumbus (monitor lizards) to climb forts, and interact the skills with birds. Spies will have to wear a silver ring, the back of which will have the Chola tiger mudra. The tiger with one line indicates an entry-level spy, two lines indicate a mid-level a spy and three lines indicate a spy leader.

'The spies can take any form any time—sometimes as loaders, traders, Vedic pandits, barbers, etc. They merge with the crowds so that they do not get noticed. For example, if a spy is standing as a mahout, people will notice the elephant and not the mahout. He can perform any role without being noticed by anyone.

'In a crowd watching a drama, a spy should not operate as a drama artist as people will see them, whereas they should act as loaders and other supporting workers so that they do not get noticed.

'We also teach them how to sound like a bird and an animal. When your co-spy shouts like an owl to reveal his location, then your response should not be like that of an owl as people may be able to figure out. Instead, you should sound more like a parrot. We try to teach such a secret language to our spies.

'We carry messages through pigeons. We write messages on a thin long silk cloth, and condense it into a small roll. The spies are also taught how to extract a message from the body of the pigeons.

'We have so many techniques to extract information from the enemy country and send the same to our kingdom. Please note we also have internal spying systems through which our ruler gets feedback on so many internal Chola bureaucracies. Our ruler will have multichannels of the spy network. For example, he may know now, where I'm giving a lecture and about what. Such is the power of our spy network, my dear boys.

'Understand boys, anyone interested in becoming a spy, may take the elective subject Spy Network of the Cholas and spend a year in this spy school. Any questions?'

The whole class was spellbound, mesmerized by the spying techniques of the Chola kingdom. Surya came up with a question.

'Namaskar Guruji, you said we had to use the spy network against enemies. In today's context who are the potential enemies of the Chola kingdom?'

'A very intelligent question. I can see the traits of military leadership in you by your question.

'We have the Chalukya kingdom divided into east and west. The eastern Chalukyas support us and our ruler Raja Raja's daughter Kundavai is married to their King Vimaladitya. But western Chalukyas now headed by Jayasimha keep troubling the east Chalukyas and thereby the Cholas. He is enemy number one.

'We have not captured the glittering crown and regal jewels deposited by the Pandyas fifty years ago with the Lankan king, Mahinda. He is our enemy number two. We need to complete this unfinished agenda.

'Raja Raja Chola conquered the Pandyas but the conquered Pandya king Amar Bhujarga is waging guerrilla wars from the forests. He is enemy number three.

'Our ruler destroyed the fleet of the Chera King Bhaskara Ravi Varman in the Kandalur war. He drove away the tantric Chera Brahmins, Rava Dasa and a few others who cunningly killed Aditya Karikala. The Chera Brahmins are regrouping with their cunning methods. They are our enemy number four.

My dear boy, these are the enemy targets that we know

as of today. But as we move on in our life, new enemies might crop up. We need to be vigilant at all times.

'Stay hungry, stay vigilant, serve the Chola army, my dear boys! Good luck.'

Krishna Raman's words reverberated in the minds of the boys for a long time. He left an indelible mark in their minds.

27

Kaliyuga, year 4110 (AD 1010), Sadhya Thirunal (Sadhya Star Day), Chitra month; the Brihadishvara temple in Thanjavur, 250th day of the ruler Raja Raja Chola and the twenty-fifth year of his reign

In the next twenty-five days, the grand temple would be dedicated to the whole world. Last-minute work was going on in full swing and the area was too busy.

The temple was emerging as the most beautiful specimen of Tamil culture remarkable for its stupendous proportions and for the simplicity of its design. A rectangular court 750 feet by 250 feet is divided into two by a wall, which carries a low tower of beautiful design. The inner court is twice as long as the outer.

The chief shrine occupies the centre of the western half of the inner court and the vimana (spire of the temple) which rises over the sanctum to a height of nearly two hundred feet on a square base of about hundred feet, dominates the whole structure.

There are decorative motifs and graceful sculptures on the side of the vimana. Numerous inscriptions that carry the history of the Cholas are carved on the walls.

The shadow of the tower cannot be seen from any angle. The wonderful structure is pleasing and mesmerizing. Colossal amounts of resources have gone into the making of this mammoth temple. A huge quantity of sand holds the foundation. It can withstand earthquake of any magnitude. A large quantity of granite from different parts of the kingdom and its neighbours was brought for this construction.

Karuvur Devar, a celebrated hymnist, saint and guru of Raja Raja Chola, was the mastermind behind this great work.

The boys of the army school were taken to the temple dedicated to the kingdom. They were ecstatic. A strange thing happened, when they were taking a round.

28

There was a huge crowd of people, some of them giving last-minute touches to the sculptures and some of the public viewing the grandiose finishes.

The boys went round the temple, some of them climbing up the huge wall out of curiosity. Different floors of the tower were closed for the public. On the eighth floor, Raja Raja Chola was inspecting the progress of the sculptures which were given finishing touches.

Surya was curious. He thought that there was a chance to have a glimpse of the ruler from close quarters. Of course, he had spent time with Rajendra Chola but not Raja Raja Chola. He decided to sneak inside the tower, when the security personnel were moving to the other side. He did succeed in his attempt, as fate favoured him to move closer to the ruler.

It was a great mistake to sneak inside, breaking the security cordon, but the boy's mind was only focused on seeing Raja Raja Chola from close quarters, nothing else registered in his mind.

From a distance on the eighth floor, Surya saw Raja Raja Chola. He was inspecting a sculpture on the outside of the vimana. His heart pumped as he went closer.

At that time, he saw a middle-aged lady wearing a monk's dress. *Perhaps she is a Buddhist nun*, he thought. *What would a Buddhist do in a Shiva temple?* a thought flashed in his mind.

While he was thinking, he saw the lady was moving fast.

Surya realized that she was probably going to push the ruler from behind from the eighth floor. The ruler was busy talking to the sculptor enquiring about the sculpture.

Surya did not waste a second. He moved faster and pushed the ruler to the left at the floor level.

The lady, unable to control her momentum fell flat on her face from the eighth floor onto the outer side of the temple and died on the spot.

There was chaos all around with people running here and there.

29

A huge security breach! A dent in the Chola pride! How could an enemy enter the city and make an attempt to kill the ruler right in front of the array of military forces operating there?

Surya did not think about any after-effects. He knew he had saved Raja Raja Chola, adored by the people of the kingdom. The boy did not realize the kind of interrogation he will be put to.

The ruler, when he was pulled towards the left did not realize that someone was running to push him from behind. He came to his senses. Being old, his physical reflexes had slowed down. He turned and saw a boy and then the Buddhist lady falling down. He could sense that there was an attempt to kill him.

Rajendra Chola, Krishna Rajan, the Thanjavur city guard head, senior commanders had all cordoned off the place. A flash investigation started.

The crown prince was angry.

'Thanthaiyare (Father), I have been telling you to take rest and not to strain yourself too much. You have worked enough for our Chola kingdom. Now see what happened? Right in front of our eyes this happened. I am ashamed that despite such illustrious military forces around, the enemy was able to sneak into this impregnable fort of ours.'

Krishna Raman added, 'We will thoroughly investigate. Who is this boy? Who gave him the access? Who is this nun who was able to get so close to our ruler? How did the security allow? I want to know all the facts right here.'

He shouted at the commanders of the different forces who had assembled there.'

Raja Raja Chola slowly came out of shock. A detailed investigation followed while the ruler took rest in his room at the temple. He will not come out of the temple till the temple is inaugurated, that was a vow he had taken along with Guru Karuvur Devar.

The investigation revealed startling facts.

30

Since the crown prince knew Surya, he asked him what happened. As Surya narrated, the attention turned towards the nun.

It was learnt she was Sister Vajira. She came to Chudamani Vihara in Nagapattinam from Lanka six months ago. Chudamani Vihara was headed by none other than Raja Raja Chola's daughter who had converted to Buddhism.

What?! A staunch Shaivaite ruler's daughter had converted to Buddhism? Surya thought. He got the answer soon.

Krishna Raman chipped in, 'Madevadigal, the second daughter of Raja Raja Chola was once suffering from manjal kamalai (jaundice) when she was twelve. The condition was serious. The doctors of the palace could not cure her. At that time, a Buddhist monk from Lanka wandering in the Chola kingdom applied some leaves on her, which he had brought from Lanka once. Within a few days she was normal.

'Some natural cure from nature's gift, but Madevadigal concluded that she was cured by Lord Buddha. Against all advice, she converted to Buddhism.

'Raja Raja Chola who is very tolerant about religious matters gave a place in Nagapattinam port to the Srivijaya king to construct Chudamani Vihara. Hence, he did not stop her in pursuing what she wanted.

'She became a Buddhist nun and the enemies—Lankans and others pepped her up and made her the head of Chudamani

Vihara, Nagapattinam. I warned the ruler many times that this will send a wrong signal. He did not listen.'

Rajendra Chola intervened, 'But what about this Lankan nun? How did she manage to come so close within the inner circles of my father?'

'Yes, we checked up on her. She is Sister Vajira. It seems to be the work of Mahinda. We defeated him at the war. He ran away to the jungles of Rohana with the Pandya crown and regal jewels. We thought he would remain quiet, but the silent dog has shown his dirty tricks. He planted her to carry out this mission. It apparently appears to be a suicide mission. The lady was brainwashed to take it up.'

Krishna Raman continued.

'But Minister, how could she get close to our king? That is my question.'

'Crown Prince, that lady visited your younger sister Madevedigal in the Chudamani Vihara. She said that she is studying the resemblances in the sculptural artwork of Buddhism and Shaivism. As you are aware, she blindly trusts anyone, so she gave a recommendation to our king and introduced sister Vajira her to our king.'

'But how did our king believe her?'

'Yes, Crown Prince, that is the power of talking. While comparing the religious sculptures and artwork, sister Vajira was praising Shaivaite art and gave the impression that she was more attracted towards Shaivaites. Our king is in the spiritual phase of his life nowadays, his soul is so pure, he does not even think of such evil schemes. He believed her and was very enthusiastic in describing the artwork in the temple. She used that opportunity and got close to his inner circles.'

'Minister, it is time that I get into the steps of a co-regent and govern the country. It is better to be prepared, as my father is getting old. I am also not young any more. Being in the mid-forties, I do not want to continue only as a crown prince. Let me take on the responsibilities.'

'Yes, Crown Prince, the ruler has already made up his mind in this regard. He told me that first we complete the temple, next we designate you as a co-regent. Both of you are on the same page.'

Both of them went to Raja Raja Chola and explained what happened. A major blow to the kingdom was averted by the grace of Lord Brihadishvara.

The king came to know of Surya and told his son to take care of him as he wanted Surya to hold responsible positions in the years ahead. Raja Raja Chola embraced Surya, wished him and gave a gift to him. 'Surya, I am gifting you two well-trained message-carrying pigeons: Ajili and Gujili. They will be your companions in future wars. These were gifted to me by the Caliph Al Qadir, Caliphate of Baghdad. These are the pigeons of Arabia.'

Rajendra Chola then narrated how Surya saved him mid-sea near Rameshwar. He assured his father that the boy's destiny seems to have been more integrated with the Chola rulers. He added that Surya was on the right track and he was personally monitoring his progress. Surya's royal bond continued to get even stronger.

31

Many events happened over the years. In the Kaliyuga year AD 1010 on the 275th day of the twenty-fifth year of Raja Raja Chola, the Brihadishvara temple was dedicated to public. In the Kaliyuga year 4112 (1012 AD), Rajendra Chola became co-regent thereby formally associating himself with his father in the administration of the whole Chola empire.

On day twenty-nine, Markazhi month, Kaliyuga 4114 (AD 1014), the Chola kingdom lost their beloved ruler, Raja Raja Chola.

Amidst these events in the Kaliyuga 4115 (AD 1015), Surya completed his military course, as he turned sixteen.

It was his graduation day and some leading announcements of direct placements in the senior military leadership were awaited.

Surya's parents were also amongst the audience. Rajendra Chola gave the convocation address. As a part of his speech, the following announcements were made:

- Manukesari, the son of Rajendra Chola, would take over the administration of the Chera kingdom called Sundara Keralan after his graduation along with Surya.
- Arul Mozhi, Vetri, Selvan and Surya became royal commanders (dalapathy) and the chief commanders of the cavalry, spy network force, weaponry and navy, respectively.

- Li Yuang became the deputy commander (Uba dalapathy) under Surya in the navy.

The announcements continued for all other twenty-five students who were graduating from the the Royal School of the Chola army.

There were congratulations all around and Surya was ecstatic. He will work under Navy Chief Commander Soman.

Further, Surya was ecstatic to know that Sundara Keralan was the head of the Chera kingdom. He was proud of him. His parents were proud of Surya.

Surya was now the royal commander of the Chola navy, his father was sharing this great news with everyone.

The marine war journey of Surya commenced.

Soon, he realized that he had to take on more challenges than he had thought.

PART V

The Lanka Expedition

32

Kaliyuga 4117 (AD 1017)

Rajendra Chola's consultative council (mantri sabha) meeting was on. He was reviewing the Lankan situation.

'Mantri Krishna Raman, we have yet to capture the royal crown and regal jewels of the Pandyas. They are still with the Lankan king. For more than sixty years, two of my predecessors could win wars against Lankans but could not bring the royal ornaments back. This cannot go on forever. I want to complete this unfinished agenda. That will be the starting point of my expedition, post accession to this throne.'

'Yes, Your Majesty, I agree.'

'What is the situation in Lanka now?'

'We conquered the northern part of Lanka during your father's time. Anuradhapura was conquered by us. King Mahinda ran away to the jungles of southern Lanka. In the north, the territories controlled by us, Lankan forces are regrouping.'

'This time I do not want to leave Mahinda—he not only has the prestigious regal jewels of Pandya won by us but he also tried to kill my father. He has to be taught a lesson. Why don't we go up to the southern part of Lanka and ruin him?'

'No, Your Majesty, the southern terrain is unfamiliar to us. It is full of forests with no proper access. We will lose many of our forces,' Krishna Raman advised.

'Then what do we need to do to finish Lanka and bring it under our control.'

Krishna Raman said, 'Let me suggest one thing: We attack Mahinda directly. He is re-establishing himself in Anuradhapura, as he has recaptured a part of it. I suggest, Your Majesty, you may lead the fight from the front.'

'Right, let me leave for the battle. Let Commander Soman and his team support me in the war, as he is stationed in the southern sea.'

'Your Majesty, I will stay in the capital, our Crown Prince Rajathi Raja will oversee this city. You have designated your other son to take charge of the Pandya and Chera kingdoms under our control. We will take care here. Jai Vijaye Bhava!'

Rajendra Chola started moving his forces to Lanka…

33

Anuradhapura

A part of Anuradhapura was under the control of Mahinda. He had recaptured the eastern part of the city after Rajendra Chola, who had himself led the battle, left the control to his commanders.

Once he came to know this, Rajendra Chola said, 'Where is Mahinda? We attack the fort straightaway, Soman.'

The Chola forces ransacked the city. The Lankan army could not bear the onslaught of the 2,00,000-strong Chola army. The Lankan army surrendered. The fort where Mahinda stayed was under siege.

Rajendra Chola said, 'Soman, this time you will not leave Mahinda. I will not leave Lanka until I capture the regal jewels.'

'Yes, Your Majesty. Our forces have entered the fort, we are searching all over. But we are unable to trace Mahinda and his family. He seems to have escaped again,' Soman said.

'Oh, no I cannot take it again. Even if he goes to any part of Lanka, I will chase him, track him down.'

Meanwhile, Surya who was attached to Commander Soman walked in with a message.

'What is this message, Surya?' Soman asked.

Surya said, 'We have captured Keerthi, the minister of Mahinda.'

'Bring him here, let me talk to him,' Rajendra Chola intervened.

'Yes, he will come here in a short while,' Surya replied.

Keerthi, was soon brought in by the Chola guards.

'Pranam, Your Majesty. I surrender to you, but I cannot say a word about Mahinda.'

'We will tear you into pieces. Behave yourself!' Rajendra Chola stopped him.

'Anyway, even if I say anything, you are going to kill me or jail me. What do I gain?' Keerthi asked.

Rajendra Chola looked into his eyes and said, 'What do you want? We know about you Keerthi. You are the one who designed this Anuradhapura fort as well as a secret fort in Rohana in the southern forest of Lanka. Nothing is free in life. I intend to create a new capital city away from our present capital, Thanjavur. Our capital city is filled with too many non-Cholas, as we brought people from all over for constructing our grand temple there. Moreover, we cannot cross river Cauvery and its tributaries during floods with our elephants and horses for our battles taking place in the northern region of our kingdom. I want to create the new capital city addressing all these issues. I would like to create an impregnable city. It will serve as the capital for all generations to come. Considering your expertise in designing cities, I can offer you the prestigious position of "New Capital City Development Minister". This position will will entail all the ministerial powers. Don't lose an excellent opportunity and get yourself killed in fighting for this useless king who is a coward running away from battles. Are you ready to take up this challenge?'

34

The ice was broken. Surya was observing the tactical brain of his ruler from close quarters.

After initial reluctance, Keerthi agreed to spill the beans.

'Now that you are giving a great importance to my skills, I accept your offer, Your Majesty. I will use all my expertise and create your new capital city over the next few years. The city will be like that of Dwarka created by Viswakarma for Lord Krishna.

'Let me tell you the secrets. Mahinda, his queen and daughter along with the crown and regal jewels you're looking for escaped via the underground secret tunnel in the eastern side of the palace. He left for Rohana, the southern forest capital, the moment you entered Lanka. By now they might have even reached.

'His two-year-old son has been given to an unknown ordinary servant who left for an undisclosed location. An ordinary servant was selected for bringing up his son because he wanted his son to be safe. I do not know where his son has been taken to.

'Soman, what do we do now?' Rajendra Chola asked his general.

'Your Majesty, can I humbly say something here?' Surya chipped in.

'Surya, stop entering into the conversation of seniors. You are too young for this,' Soman tried to stop him.

'No, no, Soman, do not stop new ideas. The young generation is our future. Surya is a child prodigy. He thinks far beyond his age. Come on, Surya, what do you want to say?'

'Your Majesty, can we take this Keerthi into confidence at the first meeting? How do we know he is not a cheat like his ruler?'

'Young boy, the question is valid. Anyway you are going to kill me. What is wrong in giving me a chance? If you feel I am bluffing, you are free to kill me,' Keerthi replied.

'Your Majesty, if we are confident about him then I have a suggestion. Sometimes intrigues are better than the real battle. Without losing our resources, we have to win a war sometimes. Now the terrain is a complex one and we will be new to this new terrain of forests. Hence, it is better to save our energy and win with our brains without draining our resources.'

'So, what is your suggestion?'

'Yes, Your Majesty, I am coming to that. We can ask Keerthi to go over to the southern capital via the same underground tunnel and represent to Mahinda that he negotiated for a peace treaty with the Chola ruler. He can say that he gave a cunning proposal to the Chola king by which the Chola kingdom will restore the rule of Mahinda in Lanka. Lanka will pay annual tributes, as determined by the Cholas. And the Cholas will agree to waive the return of the crown and the regal jewels.

'Once he convinces Mahinda about this forthcoming non-existing treaty, he will agree to come down and meet you to sign it. This gains credence once the message is carried by his own minister Keerthi.

'Once he is brought here on the pretence of signing the

treaty, we will imprison him and get what we want.'

'Brilliant idea, Surya. Now you see, Soman, why I insist we should listen to the young ones,' Rajendra Chola concluded.

However, the implementation of the idea was not as easy as it was thought out to be.

35

The next day Rajendra Chola told Soman that it was better if only Surya were to go with Keerthi. It was not advisable for the commander to go to the opponent's location.

He advised both Keerthi and Surya: 'Both of you note one thing. Surya should be presented as Crown Prince Rajathi Raja. Mahinda has not seen the crown prince since he is taking control of our kingdom from the capital city and he has not visited Lanka yet. That ruse will help them better. Surya, this is a risky covert operation. Take care.'

'Your Majesty, we will follow your guidelines. I will be careful in this operation. We will come out successful after this operation,' Surya assured Rajendra Chola.

Both bid goodbye and proceeded to Rohana through the underground tunnel from the palace. But Surya was wondering why the ruler asked him to present himself as the crown prince. Anyway he decided to focus on Mission Mahinda. The underground tunnel was big enough to accommodate horses. They were carrying oil lamps.

After travelling through the tunnel which ended in a gate, they reached a small fort palace.

'From here, we will have to travel further into the forest,' said Keerthi.

It was a dense forest. The different sounds of birds and animals were heard in the background. The tall trees with dense leaves with sighting of wild animals were a great sight to watch. *Had it not been for this mission, I would love to spend some time in the forest*, Surya thought.

But it was a tough terrain. The forest sometimes went through the mountains, sometimes the rough paths were going up or deep down in it. The valley had a number of lakes, filled with rainwater from the mountain tops. It was a 360-degree panoramic view from the top—forests, trees, lakes and the greenery.

But at times the roads were slippery. *It would have been a disaster had we moved our forces through this jungle*, he thought. *We would have had considerable loss of life, since the terrain is new. The opponent, knowing the terrain better, will always have an advantage over us.*

After two days of travel, they reached the fort located on the mountain. The fort was well-constructed.

'Anatdivipa Durga it is an island fort, a unique fort surrounded by water bodies. The design was made by me,' Keerthi said.

'Now, you have a water fort, I am seeing it for the first time.'

'The enemy cannot enter this fort, it is a strongly fortified town. We have allowed crocodiles a free rein in the water. At least twenty-five crocodiles are there in the lake.

'There is a watchtower guarding the roads and passes the whole day and night. The impregnable fortress has been the safest destination for Mahinda. He can withstand a siege inside this fort for months together, as there are enough grains stored there. There is a full-fledged town inside.

'Had you all decided to lay siege to this fort, it would be a problem not for Mahinda but for you. First of all, bringing a large force into this terrain is difficult. He has set landmines at some pathways, deep pits are camouflaged with leaves. The elephants, horses and men will fall into these and get trapped.

'Even if you cross and reach here, your forces will starve but not Mahinda as he has enough stocks inside. Hence, it was a wonderful decision to have a war of intrigue rather than a real military battle.'

'As we are on the banks of the lakes surrounding the fort, we are being watched by the clock tower.'

'How do we go inside?'

'Wait, you see now the beauty of the fort.'

There were decorative poles every two feet, which were connected by the ornamental chains. It is beautification well as a protective mechanism, Surya thought.

An interesting thing happened at that time...

36

Keerthi pulled the ornamental chain connecting the poles located across the lake. He pulled it twice. There was some noise inside the fort. It resembled a bell ringing twice: 'Ding, dong'.

It was a surprise, the window of the watchtower opened and Keerthi gave some peculiar sign, namely, 'jumping twice'.

Suddenly, a boat came from the other side of the shore where they were standing. Keerthi and Surya got into the boat. 'See how the boat is rowed in this crocodile-infested lake? We should take care when launching or retrieving the boats. Avoid standing in the boat when moving on water. Do not lean over the water from boats since the crocodiles are known to launch their entire body length out of the water in an attempt to catch their prey. Stay careful.'

Keerthi was taking lessons on how to handle crocodiles. They reached the banks of the fort. The gates opened. Two guards took them to the palace hall located inside the fort.

Both were asked to take a seat. Mahinda walked in; he was surprised to see Keerthi. However, he greeted him warmly.

'Keerthi, why are you here? I told you to be there in Anuradhapura and live secretively. That will enable us to regroup later, once Rajendra Chola leaves. He cannot stay permanently in Lanka.'

'No, Your Majesty, I have successfully brokered a deal with Rajendra Chola,' Keerthi said.

'What kind of a deal? By the way, who is this young man with you?'

'Your Majesty, he is none other than the crown prince of Chola kingdom—Rajathi Raja.'

'What? Come again, is he the crown prince? Why and how did you bring him here?

'Your Majesty, I have arranged for a treaty to be signed by you and the Cholas in which we agree to give annual tributes to the Cholas of a sum to be determined by them. They will restore your rule in Lanka and also give up their claim to the Pandya's regal jewels under your custody. This is the best deal. Why do you live like a prisoner in this godforsaken place, Your Majesty? I have come here to take you to your capital where Rajendra Chola is waiting.'

'The deal seems to be fine. But how can I believe Rajendra Chola? He may imprison me. I cannot believe him without adequate protection. The Chola king is so serious about it which is why he has sent his son here.

'But I still feel there is some catch here. I do not want to get trapped. Moreover, now you have shown our place of hiding to the Cholas.'

'Your Majesty, to add credibility to what we say, I the crown prince of the Cholas will stay here till you get what you want,' Surya chipped in.

'Yes, this seems to be a workable deal. I agree, let this young man stay here under the watchful eyes of my guards. Keerthi, let me take my wife and daughter along. Come let us go.'

Keerthi, Mahinda, his wife and daughter left Rohana fort for Anuradhapura to meet the Chola ruler, leaving Surya behind.

37

As they left, Surya was alone in that isolated place where there were a few guards. He got up early the next day and thought of swimming in the lake.

Crocodiles came to his mind. A few cautions learnt during his 'fort capture technique classes' came to his mind:

- Crocodiles are most dangerous at dusk, as they prefer mornings for swimming.
- Avoid swimming in crocodile-infested waters during their mating and breeding sessions when they are most active. In the southern side, Aadi and Avani (July and August) are the only seasons.
- Try to swim below the water surface to avoid splashing which may attract crocodiles.
- The eyes of the crocodile are the most vulnerable part, hence attempt to gouge, kick or poke the animal in their eyes as a survival technique.
- Also, the next part to hit is the head of the crocodile, for survival.
- Do not put yourself in a position to be taken by a crocodile in the first place.

What a great military training our Chola kingdom gave to us, Surya thought and admired his school as they had simulated every single situation that they may face in an enemy/war zone. Remembering all the techniques he learnt, Surya decided to swim in the lake to freshen himself up.

He jumped into the water. He kept moving under it, as he could stay underwater even for three consecutive days at a stretch. He kept his ears close to the water and listened to the movement signals of the species underwater. He had the special ability to see underwater, keeping his eyes wide open.

As he was swimming, he spotted a closed ornamental pot under the water. *Why is an ornamental pot lying underwater?* Surya wondered. He swam towards it. One crocodile was sitting over it. He realized he should kill it and move the box quickly. If he delayed his exit, he may be surrounded by other crocodiles. He had to be quick!

He decided to use a sharp knife to gouge the crocodile's eyes. Once the eyes were hit badly the crocodile was shocked for a second. At the point, Surya strongly hit its head. The crocodile died. Immediately, he took the pot and swiftly swam towards the fort underwater without splashing. Quickly he reached the fort.

Once in his room he opened the pot.

'The royal crown glittering spotless with the aaram and the necklace!'

Surya's joy had no boundaries. The whole purpose of the Lankan war was over.

He had to move out quickly. His horses were on the other side of the lake. The guards did not worry much, as they thought that Surya could not move out of the fort, as there were no boats left in the fort. They did not know that Surya could walk on water up to hundred yards. Surya used his special skills, carried the pot, walked on the water carefully avoiding crocodiles, reached his horses and moved towards Anuradhapura.

38

Anuradhapura

The palace was active again as Keerthi, Mahinda, his wife and daughter arrived. The Lankan people were celebrating his arrival, wrongly assuming he had won the war.

The palace hall witnessed the great meeting between the Cholas and the Lankans.

'Your Majesty, as promised, I have convinced our Lankan king about the treaty and brought him here. Now the treaty can be signed. As a confidence-building measure, Crown Prince Rajathi Raja stayed back at the Rohana fort.'

'Oh, Crown Prince is in Rohana in the safe custody of Mahinda. Till now Mahinda was only holding the regal jewels of the Pandyas for the last two generations. Now has he taken to holding the crown prince in safe custody? By the way, where are the crowns and the regal jewels? Has he brought them with him?'

'Hey, Chola King, what are you talking? You have agreed to waive your rights on the Pandya crown and regal jewels. Why are you not respecting the treaty? By the way, your son Rajathi Raja is with me in Rohana. Don't forget,' Mahinda shouted back at Rajendra Chola.

'What treaty? Do not daydream Mahinda. How can you expect the Chola empire to sign a treaty with a defeated king like you? You are good for nothing. Your fate is in my hands. Guards, arrest him, his wife and daughter,' Rajendra Chola said.

The guards arrested and handcuffed them. And then they were paraded in public with their handcuffs on. To let the Lankans know that the whole of Lanka was now subservient to Chola rule.

'Hey, Chola, you are crossing your limits. By imprisoning me, you will not get your royal crown and the regal jewels back. But your crown prince will not return. Your Chola army will feel the heat. They will start murmuring for the regal jewels, the king has made his crown prince the scapegoat.'

'Stop talking, Mahinda. Your days are over. Surya, my commander who came to you as the crown prince has already sent a message through his companion pigeon Ajili that the crown and regal jewels were retrieved from below the water of the lake surrounding your fort. He is well on his way.'

'Oh no! He has retrieved the jewels. Hey Keerthi, you are also a traitor, let me instigate the Lankans to revolt against the Chola rule. Every Lankan living here will lay down a trap for the Cholas. You cannot keep one soldier for monitoring each Lankan citizen. The governance cannot happen if the people do not cooperate. You will face the agitating Lankan public soon.'

'Mahinda, now your minister Keerthi is on my side. But he himself did not know the whereabouts of the regal jewels. My special skilled commander caught hold of these treasures. Soman take this fellow, his wife and daughter to Thanjavur. Let him stay imprisoned till the end of his life. Let me see his prison cell from my palace every day. He tried to kill my father. He deserves this punishment. Let us not kill him. If we kill him, he will become a martyr for his people. A falling seed creates a vriksham. Do not make a martyr out of a monkey.

Let him be imprisoned forever.'

'Where is your son, Kasibha? I will also put him in jail with you. Let your whole family stay forever?'

'Hey, Chola, you cannot find my son. Try if you can. What you do now is going to hit you back one day.'

Mahinda shouted back.

Rajendra Chola appointed his son Chola Langeswaran to oversee the Lankan province under Chola rule.

He moved back to his home in Thanjavur with the prisoners, Mahinda, his wife and daughter and the royal crown, mythical aaram and the pearl jewels.

Once he reached his capital city he made sure that Mahinda and his family were placed under house arrest in a palace house right in front of his palace.

Later, a startling revelation was made, which astonished Rajendra Chola.

PART VI

The Ganga Expedition

39

High from his victory, Rajendra Chola wanted to have a big celebration in Thanjavur. He thought of presenting a caged Mahinda in front of public.

Surya placed the cage in front of Mahinda.

'Hey, are you the one who impersonated your crown prince? Are you not ashamed of cheating? It is not raj dharma. Don't you know that?'

'Oh, deflated king, still your ego is at a high altitude. You teach us about raj dharma. You are the man who ran away from the battlefield and hid yourself like a mouse inside a hole. You denied us the regal jewels won by us from the Pandyas. You have no right to talk about raj dharma.

'We are going to present you in this cage to our public showing you as the animal that tried to murder our beloved ruler Raja Raja Chola, the great. We will tell them you are the rat that tried to hide in a hole. Wait, your ego will be decimated. Still you have not lost your false pride. Mind you, you are in the Chola kingdom, not Lanka.'

'Stop it, you fraudulent man. The regal jewels you captured are imitations. I had safely sent the real jewels out of Lanka, as soon as your ruler Rajendra landed in Lanka. You have imprisoned me, find out where are the real jewels if you can. What will you celebrate with imitation jewels? You underestimated Mahinda.'

Surya was astonished to hear this. He immediately rushed

to the ruler with this message. The authenticity of the jewels was tested by the jewellers of the Chola kingdom. Yes, they turned out to be fake.

Then came the famous anger of Rajendra Chola. He did not get angry easily, but once he did, it was difficult to face it. The whole capital city felt it the next day.

40

Rajendra Chola was upset. The effect of it was felt in the meetings with ministers.

Rajendra Chola ordered for an expert team who deal with the most violent criminals and extract vital information from them.

The team assembled at the jail palace of Mahinda. Rajendra Chola too was present. His repeated requests to Mahinda could not elicit any answer.

The torture began—right in the early morning when Mahinda was sleeping. Cold water was splashed on his face. He was kept at neck-deep water throughout the day and night with no food. He could not sleep, he pleaded for help. None came for any help.

Next morning, he was taken out of the water, laid on the floor. Two guards beat him repeatedly on his feet and toes. Mahinda was feeling giddy. His body was aching, the pain was spreading, he and was crying, 'Aiyo, aiyo.'

Still he refused to reveal where he had hidden the royal crown and the regal jewels. Rajendra Chola ordered the torture to continue in front of his wife and daughter. That did the trick.

Mahinda's wife cried uncontrollably. She could not see her husband facing such intense torture.

She cried, 'Please stop the torture. I will tell the truth. The regal jewels have been sent through the traders moving to Vangala (Bengal) Desa. They were deposited with King

Mahipala of the Pala dynasty for safe custody on a special request from my husband. They have been close friends since there has been an exchange of trade through the sea over the past several generations. You got what you want, now please leave my husband.'

'You may note if the information is false, your husband will be subjected to torture every day.'

'No, why should I lie? What is the point in hiding the truth,' the Lankan replied in a soft broken voice.

'You said it right, you have a quick grasp of the situation,' Rajendra Chola said and walked away.

The next day the raj darbar witnessed several resolutions and new agendas. The noise from the war bugles was reverberating all over the capital city of the Cholas.

41

Raj Darbar

Rajendra Chola addressed the gathering: 'We have come to know that the regal jewels captured from the Lankans are fake. We also now know that these were deposited with Mahipala of Vangala Desa (Bengal), the lineage of the Pala dynasty. Mahipala has been colluding with Jayasima of the Chalukyas and gave trouble to my sister Kundavi and nephew Raja Narendra. He is already our enemy, now he has become a confirmed enemy, and we have to attack Mahipala right at his doorstep. What do you think, Krishna Raman?'

'The vision is clear, Your Majesty. We will look at an action plan. To reach Mahipala, we have to cross several countries, some of which are close to him, and some are neutral to the both of us. The kingdoms include:

- Vengi—under our ally Raja Narendra;
- West Chalukya—ruled by Jayasimha, our biggest enemy;
- Chakara Kottam—ruled as a province of Jayasimha, Chalukya;
- Odda Desha—ruled by a neutral king Indra Dutta, his allegiance is not clear;
- Dhandabukti—ruled by Dharmapala, a king who obeys Mahipala;

- Dakshina Lada—ruled by Rana Sura, a close ally of Mahipala;
- Kosala Desha—ruled by Govinda Chandra, a Brahmin ruler, always fearing for Mahipala; and
- Vangala De (Uthra Lada)—ruled by our enemy target Mahipala.'

'Your Majesty, piercing into all these kingdoms will involve a great deal of time and resources. Further, their language and the climate are totally alien to us. We have to carefully plan this military campaign.'

'Krishna Raman, first, do we have our spy network in place in all these places under a regional single-point control? We need free flow of information. We should know the details of our enemy before we attack them. What is your spy network arrangement?'

'Your Majesty, we have house spies disguised as Brahmins, leaders, traders, barbers, singers, cattle-breeders and so on. They may change their roles depending upon the situation. But all this information will converge to a regional controller who himself is in a disguise. The regional controllers pass on information to the main control, directly to my office. We always have information at our fingertips on our enemy targets.'

'Do not be complacent, sometimes we are also deceived at times like the episode of the fake jewels. This was never detected by us. Who are your regional controllers?'

'Your Majesty, our regional controllers are:

- Kashyap Sharma, as a pandit in Kashi (Varanasi);
- Kula Sekara, as a Buddhist monk in Lanka;
- Vardhini, as a dancer in Madurai;

- Narayana Nampoothiri, as a priest of Ananda Padmanaba Swamy temple in the Chera kingdom;
- Alwar Josier, as an astrologer in Thanjavur;
- Sima Vishnu, as a security guard of the Varadha Raja temple in Kanchipuram;
- Vaniga Vellar as a trader in Vengi;
- Between the Chalukya kingdom and to the northern Ganga provinces, various Brahmins are moving towards the Kailash mountain in the north.

We have a fairly well spread-out network, nothing to worry as far as information is concerned, Your Majesty.'

Then the discussion turned towards the war strategy, during which a shocking information was revealed by a spy from the north.

110 • THE CONQUEST OF THE EAST

The Ganga Expedition

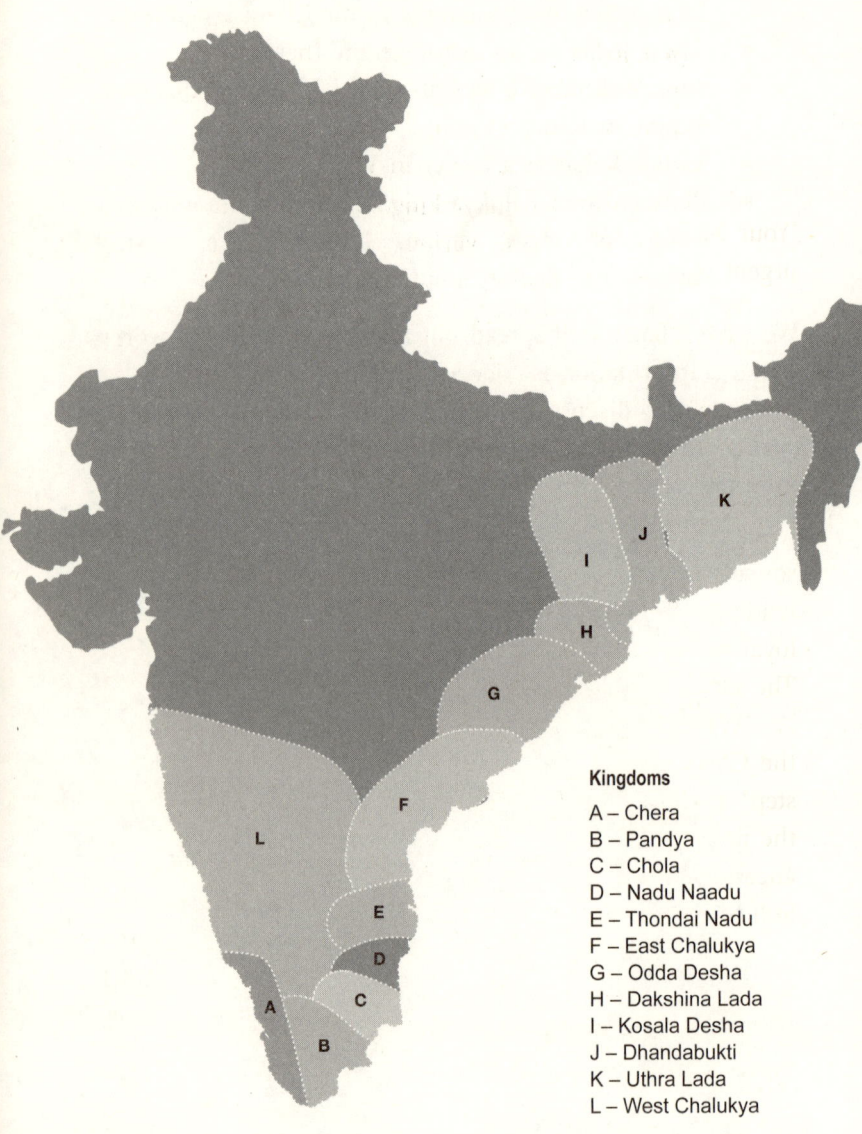

Kingdoms

A – Chera
B – Pandya
C – Chola
D – Nadu Naadu
E – Thondai Nadu
F – East Chalukya
G – Odda Desha
H – Dakshina Lada
I – Kosala Desha
J – Dhandabukti
K – Uthra Lada
L – West Chalukya

42

'Your Majesty, a few traders have come from Vengi with an urgent message.'

'What is it? Bring them in, Krishna Raman.' Rajendra Chola could not control his anxiety, as he was very attached to his nephew, Raja Narendra, currently ruling Vengi after the demise of his father Vimaladitya.

'Your Majesty, we have bad news. Raja Narendra, his queen and children have been put under house arrest. Jayasimha, the western Chalukya king has placed his puppet ruler. Vijayaditya, son of the former Vengi king and his concubine, has been made the new ruler of Vengi. The ministers and the army loyal to Raja Narendra, the deposed king, is underground. The situation is not good in Vengi, Your Majesty.'

'What? Jayasimha has so much courage to defy against the Cholas? What gave him the guts to take this audacious step? Krishna Raman, we begin our war with Vengi—throw the new ruler out and teach Jayasimha, a great lesson. Their ancestors also kept playing with us. My father punished them. Still they do not learn their lessons.'

Krishna Raman began to convey his views, 'Your Majesty, we have been talking about marching towards Mahipala's kingdom. Now we cannot delay this. First, we start to set things right in Vengi and then move towards the north. Since we understand Mahipala and also support Jayasimha, it is all the more necessary we go up to the north till the river

Ganga and defeat Mahipala on his home ground. But before that we have to ensure that the south is under firm control, so that when our forces move towards the north, we do not get problems from the south.'

'Krishna Raman, we plan it this way—Thanjavur will be under the crown prince, my son Rajathi Raja, under your guidance. The Pandya kingdom will be under Sundara Chola Pandyan, the Chera region will be controlled by Manu Kula Kesary Chola Keralan and Lanka will be under Chola Lankeswaran with Commander Soman. The thus southern region will be under close control.

'Now I myself move north with nine lakh army men and enough elephants and horses. The commander to lead will be Araiyan Rajan backed up by your son Arul Mozhi, and Miladuyar, Brahmendra, Pallavaraya, Veera Sena and Paranjothi.

'We have to use both direct war and intrigue. I do not want to lose my countrymen on wars that can be avoided.

'For direct war all the above commanders will group under Araiyan Rajan. But for war intrigues and tactical war games, Surya will accompany me.'

'Surya? He is a kid. How can we give him this war-driven intrigues? Are you sure?'

'Araiyan Rajan is not Soman, the Lanka region commander. Araiyan does not work closely with youngsters. He is an old-timer, hierarchy-focused man. He has in fact not accepted my son Arul Mozhi.'

'Look, young blood has to be infused into our military leadership. I came to power in my middle age only. I openly voiced my concern on this to my father. Only you intervened at that time and made me a co-regent during my father's life time. I have already decided to declare my son, Rajathi Raja as co-regent after this war. Youths have to be encouraged. Surya single-handedly managed Operation Rohana and brought Mahinda into our jails. Let Araiyan Rajan learn to work with the youth. Surya will report to me directly on this mission. I am going to lead this battle from the front. I will go up to the river Tungabhadra, and afterwards I will guard the boundary of Vengi from the Tungabhadra with one and a half lakh army men. Ariyan Rajan, your son Arul Mozhi and other commanders will move further north of the Tungabhadra with seven and half lakh army men.

'If I move out of Vengi, Jayasimha of Western Chalukya will create trouble. I will restore our Raja Narendra's rule, stay there till we conquer Mahipala.

'After winning the long war. I will conduct the coronation ceremony of Raja Narendra, give my daughter Anumanga in marriage to him. After solidifying the Cholas' relationship with Vengi, I will return to our capital. Till that time, Rajathi Raja and you will firmly control our headquarters. Are you clear, Rajathi Raja?'

'Yes, Appa (Father), I am listening. I believe in action. I completely agree with what you said. We will be missing you for at least one year. That is the only worry. By the way, Minister Krishna Raman, can we not take my sister and cousin out of the Vengi prison? We have forces loyal to us at Vengi, even though Jayasimha launched his puppet as a ruler there.'

Krishna Raman intervened at this stage.

43

'Rajathi Raja, you are bang on target. I examined that first. Sound it out to our spy network as well as to the Vengi forces in hiding, who are loyal to us. The information is very disturbing. Your aunt, the mother the of deposed Vengi king is creating a problem. She says, "Why should I run away like a thief? Ask my brother Rajendra Chola to come with three lakh forces and formally save me." She refused to accept any covert operation to release her and bring her back here. I am confused on this.'

'Krishna Raman, did you just say she refused to come out of a covert operation? What does she think of herself? She has always been fickle-minded. Does she think our Chola soldiers have to give away their lives for her? Is that their only job? Had she been nice and vigilant, she would not have allowed her husband to spend his life on other women and vices? That this is how Jayasimha of western Chalukya entered Vengi by the back door.'

'I am very angry. Why don't we punish her for this adamant attitude? I am tired of her. I have other work to do. I cannot spend my life protecting her. Appa, Jayasimha wants her and my cousin in his custody. He must be thinking that we will protect him from our invasion. He knows that we will be afraid that he will kill them if we invade. He is holding them hostages against us.'

'Your judgement is spot-on Rajathi Raja. You are thinking beyond your age. Raja lakshna (king's traits) is visible in you.

Let me add here, we also need your sister to be longer, as our main bond with her alone will pull Raja Narendra towards us. If he loses her, we may lose Raja Narendra also,' Krishna Raman interjected.

'So, we need her alive even though she refuses to move out. Then intrigue has to come to play over and above the direct war. Let me hand over this covert operation as a special task to Surya. Also in a week from now, I am moving with the entire eight lakh forces. I will join Arayan Rajan who is already reaching the borders of Vengi with one lakh men from our army. Let us get prepared.'

'Also, both of you note that since we go north to the banks of the river, I will bring abundant Ganga water to our new city and fill our lakes with the pure waters of the river Ganga. My father told me that he could not execute this in his lifetime and he wanted me to do it. For designing the new city, I have already appointed Keerthi, as he is an expert in city design. I call him "Viswakarma of City Construction".'

The council meeting ended with the detailed war plan and Rajathi Raja moved into action to release the resources for his father's trip to the north.

44

Vengi, the raja's court

Vimaladitya is on the throne. Jayasimha is sitting on a special chair, as he is the ruler in reality.

'Your Majesty Vengi king, Your Majesty Chalukya king, a personal emissary has come from Rajendra Chola,' the darbar man announced in a husky voice.

'Ask him to come in.'

'Your Majesty, I am Surya, a personal messenger of King Rajendra Chola. Here is the message:

Shri Jayasimha,

I do not want to start a war with you. Our earlier generations have shed enough blood on this soil. Let there be peace henceforth. I want my sister and nephew released, and I will take them back to my kingdom with me.

You can rule Vengi with your nominee with no trouble from me. For this gesture, I want you to allow a free passage to me and my soldiers across, since I want to go up to the Ganga and square up my old enmity with Mahipala on the banks of the river.

Looking forward to our good relations.

Rajendra Chola

'What! Your king is now afraid of me, he is begging me? Surya is your name—isn't it?'

'He is not begging, Your Majesty. He is asking in the name of humanity to avoid bloodshed.'

'Your king is a fool. Why should I release his kin? They are my trump card. If I release them, your king will attack me and I will have no hold on him. If they are with me, he will be afraid to attack me in the fear that I will kill them. Also, Mahipala is my ally. Why should I allow your king a safe passage to attack my ally?'

'No, Your Majesty, he was serious when he offered this proposal to you. Please think for a while. Now Vengi is divided, the people are in two camps. If their queen and their legitimate ruler Raja Narendra are in your custody, there will be public anger against you. After all, what do you really want? You want the kingdom. When it is coming to you with goodwill for releasing them as they want to go to the Chola kingdom on their own, the crowd will accept you wholeheartedly.'

Jayasimha looked into the eyes of Surya. He started taking an interest in him.

'Give me ten days to stay here with you as a diplomat, Your Majesty. During this time, I will assure you that no Chola army will march towards this kingdom. During this time, I will interact between you and our ruler. I will share your concerns and get a mutually beneficial deal struck between you two. After all, destroying your kingdoms with his nine lakh forces is not a big issue for our ruler. Also, note that no one is an ally in politics. Opportunities change the rules of the games. Who knows if you give a free passage to cross your kingdoms towards the north, our king may agree to share the valuables with you that he will win from Mahipala. All I am saying is that keep an open mind. All you need is a guarantee that the Chola will not attack you, once you release his kin. We will strike solutions. I am here right in front of you guaranteeing you that the Cholas will not do anything to upset you. Otherwise you can jail me. I have volunteered to stay in your place under your control and vigilance. What more do you want?'

The ice was broken. As the offer was so natural and sincere, Jayasimha wanted to give it a chance. Surya remained under close watch in the palace. He was given a special diplomatic badge for moving freely within the city.

But the happenings around Surya were totally different.

45

While Surya was negotiating with Jayasimha at Vengi, Rajendra Chola was moving towards Vengi with his forces, while his north-wing commander Araiyan Rajan reached some ten miles closer to Vengi.

While these marches were happening, Surya was relaxed, staying in the custody of Jayasimha. But he could roam freely in the city with his diplomatic identification, duly watched by the vigilance team of Jayasimha.

Meanwhile, a couple of pandits with an aged Brahmin couple walked into the well-guarded prison palace of the deposed King Raja Narendra and his mother Kundavi.

When they were intercepted by the guards, they said they were going to carry out Thambathi Pooja (pooja for a couple to live longer) to be performed by Raja Narendra every year. The old Brahmin and his wife accompanying them are the thambathis (couples). Raja Narendra's mother asked him to do this every year till he got married.

One of the guards said, 'Let them do pooja. As long as they do not want to step into the ruling of the country, let them at least do their poojas. Let them go in.'

The pandits and the pooja parties went inside, leaving their decorated chariot outside. They took the Lord Shiva vigraha (statue) for worship.

As they entered, they located both mother and son in a room. Surya disguised as one of the pandits spoke to Kundavi.

Chola Territories under Rajendra Chola

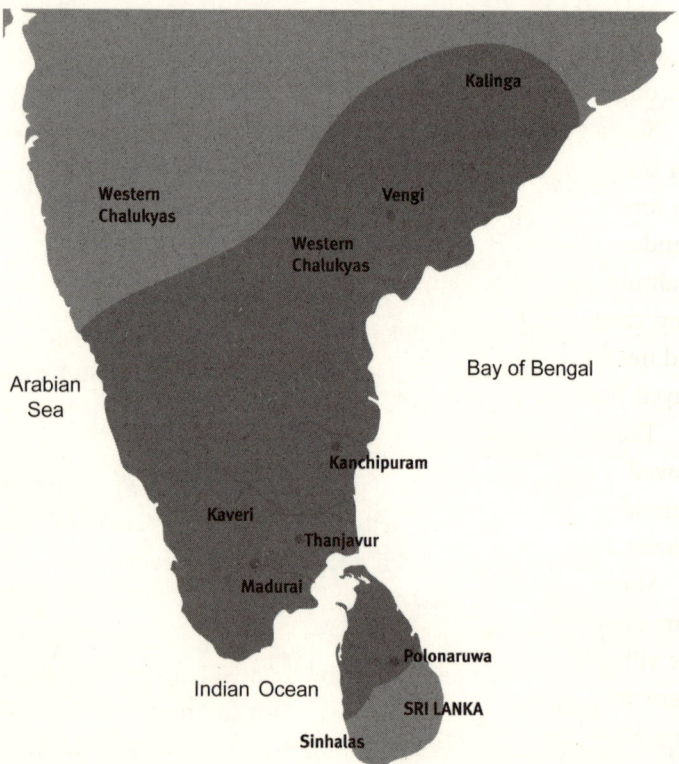

'Your Excellency, we have instructions to take you out and shift you to the border where the Chola forces are camping. Once we hand over you both to them, they will take care of you. They can begin a war only after you are handed over to them. Please get dressed like this Brahmin couple. We have to move fast. The Brahmin couple will stay here impersonating you. They have agreed to take the risk in view of their extraordinary affection for our Chola ruler. Please, we have to move fast.'

'Who are you? I am the daughter of Raja Raja Chola, the great and the sister of Rajendra Chola—the utterance of their very name will frighten the enemies. Why should I stand like a coward? I will not come out unless Jayasimha's forces are thoroughly beaten by Rajendra Chola's forces.'

Surya persuaded to the best of his abilities. But Kundavi did not budge. Then Surya had to use the authority given to him. He forcefully made her inhale the extract of green leaves and Kundavi fainted. Then they got her dressed as the traditional Brahmin lady. Raja Narendra was dressed as a pandit. Then they carried Kundavi in their arms, stating she had fainted and needed urgent medical attention. The old Brahmin couple stayed back in the prison.

The chariot carrying Kundavi, Raja Narendra and Surya moved swiftly. The pandits and the generals loyal to Raja Narendra in disguise recited Vedic hymns and followed the chariot for a few minutes and later dispersed.

Surya was intercepted once, but his diplomatic ID saved him. He said he was going to the Shiva temple in Kali Dhandhi, the village on the border of Vengi. He explained that he goes there to pay his obeisance to his family god. Kundavi and Raja Narendra were left in the custody of Chola Commander Araiyan Rajan at the border and Surya returned to his place in Vengi. What happened next was not in the favour of Surya.

46

Jayasimha made a surprise visit to the palace where the deposed Vengi king and his mother were kept as prisoners.

When he found out that they had escaped and someone else was impersonating them he got very angry and ordered their arrest.

Then the first thing that struck him was to look for Surya. He soon rushed to check on Surya.

To his surprise, he saw Surya relaxing, 'Where did you take your Chola's sister and son?'

'What? They escaped? I do not know. I promised you nothing will change during the ten-day period of our negotiations. I am surprised. I do not know anything about this. Trust me Your Majesty.' Surya was apologetic.

'Now, I will arrest you. Take him to the prison,' he thundered.

Surya was brought to the jail where there were more than 10,000 war criminals. He observed that many were from the Oddha Desha and some from the Chola kingdom as well.

It was a huge jail, housing prisoners of war. The prisoners were all stacked in multi-layered temporary beds. One hall housed at least thousand prisoners each. There were ten halls like that. Jayasimha used Vengi as the backyard for all his war prisoners. Surya became one of them. What a tragic end to the brave Surya.

While all this was happening in Vengi, Rajendra Chola reached its borders and joined Araiyan Rajan. It was a massive

Chola force of nine lakh army men.

Soon the news of Surya's imprisonment reached Rajendra Chola. He was worried for the talented boy. But he also felt that the smart young man would somehow find his way. Consoling himself, he started focusing on the war plans after safely dispatching his sister to his capital city. His nephew stayed back with him at the war front.

The next day, the massive forces attacked Vengi and conquered the palaces. They found out that Jayasimha had vacated the city with all his men, materials and money. Even the prisoners were taken with them. The palaces were empty, all the valuables were taken away, and nothing was left in the khajana (treasury).

Rajendra Chola installed his nephew Raja Narendra as the king of Vengi and left his one lakh army men with him. He ordered the forces to move north and capture Jayasimha.

The forces marched towards Chitradurga, where Jayasimha, was supposed to be hiding. The forces were fully charged, as the king himself was leading from the front.

Meanwhile, Rajendra Chola got his son Sundara Keralan, overseeing the Chera kingdom, drafted into this battle. Sundara Keralan was an expert in dealing with the river-based wars and was trained by the Chera Brahmins on de-poisoning techniques. From the spies, Rajendra Chola had got the information that some of the disgruntled elements from the Chera kingdom were being used by Jayasimha to get poison-tipped arrows for the war. No wonder Sundara Keralan, batchmate of Surya in the army school, familiar with Chera's cunning Brahmin techniques of war, was drafted into this war.

The Jayasimha camp was planning differently at the same time.

47

Chitradurga was a big commercial city of western Chalukya. At its border, Jayasimha was taking stock of the situation in his war camp.

'Senathipathy Narasimha, did Rajendra Chola start from Vengi? What is the status?'

Narasimha, was a short, stout man. There were marks of war-inflicted injuries on his face. His long moustache gave him the rakshasa look.

'Your Majesty, the Chola army is marching with nine lakh men. We have only three lakhs of our army men with us. They will decimate us.'

'Narasimha, how many war prisoners do we have?'

'We have about 50,000 prisoners, most of them Oddha Desha prisoners of war. They were captured when they invaded us in the past.'

'Will they fight for us?'

'We have to check that. We have to tempt them by saying that they can become free if they join us and fight the Cholas. I can try talking to them.'

'Do one thing, let us not burn our resources. We keep only 25,000 of our troops at the front, at the back we'll ask the 50,000 prisoners to join this fight. You head the battle.

I will move to the Masungi Fort. I have asked for support from Oddha Desha and Dakshina Lad. They may join our forces. Thus we can assemble at least half of the

Chola forces.

'Note one thing, we need to destroy half of the Chola forces before they come to Masungi, the city of snakes'.

'Yes, Your Majesty. I will lead the fight with a small army backed up by the prisoner's support here at Chitradurga.'

'If we lose this place, we will allow the Cholas to march freely without resistance. We will take backward movements. Temporally they may be happy. They may become complacent. We will also poison all the drinking water ponds in Chitradurga. Meanwhile, rains have started. River Tungabhadra will be flooded. For crossing the river, they have to construct a temporary wooden bridge. It will take a month. We move backwards till Masungi, we will remove all food and rice in the places after crossing the Tungabhadra. The tired forces of the Cholas after crossing the river will be deprived of food. Without it, they will feel weak and get more tired.

'We will also dig deep pits in the Tungabhadra River to make the surface totally uneven. When horses and elephants enter in the river, the uneven places will confuse them. They may struggle with the varying depths.

'The Chera Brahmins have come to guide us on launching poison-tipped arrows. They have brought a huge stock of paste made from poisonous leaves. As the horses and elephants struggle, the army men will try to lift them and in the meantime, our army should launch poison-tipped arrows on them from the opposite side. Soldiers will die on the spot.

'The survivors will be tired and they will be denied of their food after crossing the Tungabhadra, as we will move all the food items from the regions after the Tungabhadra

River till Musangi, where we will be waiting for them.'

'Excellent Narasimha, execute this plan, tell the prisoners immediately and convince them to fight for us.'

Jayasimha said in a hurry.

48

Narasimha, moved on to his next task. He went to the jail and presented his request.

'Namaskar to all of you, I have come here with a specific proposal from our king of Chalukyas. As you are aware, the Cholas are in our border. They have waged a war against us.

'We want you to fight for us against them. If you fight for us, we will give you money and free you after the war. What do you say?'

'If you lose against the Cholas, they will kill us. At least, we will live and be safe in the jail, Senathipathy,' a prisoner screamed.

'When we fight a war, we win. We want your support as we need additional people. Oddha Desha and Dhandabukti are sending their troops but it will take some time for them to reach. In the interim period we ask for your support. There is no reason why we should lose if we fight together against the Cholas. If we win, you are free. Even if we lose, you can always escape by telling the Cholas that you were imprisoned against your will. Unless you fight, you cannot meet them. If you refuse to fight you will all die here before meeting them.

'Will you die here now or prefer to take the chance of getting freed from our jail? Hope you will all agree.'

A prisoner asked, 'We are from the Chola kingdom, so how can you expect us to fight against our own kingdom?'

'A good question. There are only a few Cholas in this

crowd. For Chola prisoners we give more money if they fight their own men,' the senathipathy gave a counter-offer.

All the prisoners asked for one more day to give their decision.

The next day the prisoners had a chat. Surya convinced them that they should join the troops to give cover at the back of the Chalukya army stationed at the front. He also introduced himself by sharing what position he held in the Chola army. He promised them to free them, once they joined the Chalukya troops and later betrayed them by joining hands with the Cholas. He volunteered to get this done. After a few murmurs, they all gave their consent to fight for the Chalukyas. Jayasimha was very happy. He left with only about 30,000 of his troops and moved towards the Masungi Fort with his men. Narasimha, took charge of the Chitradurga palace. He had to carry out the fight with the Cholas with his limited number of men and prisoners.

49

Meanwhile, Rajendra Chola had his plans carved out. He received some tips on the opponent's strategy from his spy network. He knew about the Tungabhadra River, pits and poison-tipped arrows.

He thought of countering the strategy by calling a consultative strategy meeting with his commanders.

Chola Keralan was quick with his tactical moves. 'We will place boulders, big stones and large tree trunks in the Tungabhadra. This can arrest the water and reduce the speed and flow. The terrain after the blocks will have reduced flow and give a good view of the riverbed terrain. As the pits and potholes will be visible, we will be able to move without much strain.

'If we are hit by the poisonous arrows, we should dive immediately into water, only then the survival chances are high. Then once we get out, we can apply the anti-poisonous paste which I have brought from the Chera kingdom. This is a survival technique.'

All of them agreed on this strategy. They first attacked Chitradurga located before the Tungabhadra.

The Chola forces split into three and attacked from the north, east and west. The Chalukyas did not show much resistance, as they were small in number. To their surprise, some Chalukya troops themselves attacked their own men from the southern side. Yes, the prisoners turned against the

Chalukyas. There was chaos everywhere. The Chalukyas were jailed. Some ran away with Senathipathy Narasimha. Rajendra Chola met the prisoners and he was happy to sight Surya amongst them.

Surya narrated what happened, Rajendra Chola immediately announced that those prisoners, mostly from Oddha Desha, were free and would form a new regiment called the Oddha Chola regiment to be headed by none other than Surya himself.

Chitradurga was ransacked by the Chola troops. They took all the valuables. The king ordered some of the gold and jewels to be taken to Vengi, since their treasury was emptied by Jayasimha.

The jewels were painted black and were loaded along with other goods carried by traders on donkeys. No one knew about the valuables that were transported.

Meanwhile, that night there was a huge celebration by the Chola troops. They could take over a city with practically no resistance. Only ten Chola soldiers died against 10,000 Chalukyas.

Surya, Sundara Keralan and Arul Mozhi spent quality time together after a long time

The next morning bad news shook the Chola troops.

50

Some ponds were poisoned by the Chalukyas, who ran away from Chitradurga.

Bramendra, Miladuyar, fifty soldiers and a few sub-commanders were found dead as they swam in poisonous water. The environment suddenly turned sombre.

It was a personal loss for Surya, Sundara Keralan and Arul Mozhi. Their guru Bramendra was no more. They sobbed uncontrollably.

Rajendra Chola also felt the loss personally. Bramendra and Miladuyar were with the Chola army since his father's days. They were requested to stay back at the Royal Army School to teach children in view of their age. But they refused, saying they could not stay away from the prestigious war directly led by their king.

Fate decided otherwise. They could not see the complete victory of the Cholas.

All the bodies were cremated. Three sword scratches were made on their chests, as a as a sign of honour before they were cremated.

A Shiva linga was placed at the place of their cremation. 'Long live the Chola kingdom! Long live our ruler Rajendra Chola! Long live the martyrs!' The sound of the soldiers pierced through the skies.

Rajendra addressed:

'My fellow countrymen, no words can describe this great

loss to us. Bramendra and Miladuyar were father figures for me. All the soldiers are our men.

'We have to give it back to the Chalukyas. Go on full force against them. We have to destroy Masungi, where Jayasimha and his puppet Vijayaditya were hiding.

'Come, let me lead from the front. We will not sleep till we destroy them. I take this vow in front of the funeral fire of our countrymen, who lost their precious lives here. March ahead...'

The Chola forces moved ahead.

51

The Tungabhadra River was a few miles before the Masungi Fort. The Chola forces tried to test the water flow by sending a few elephants first into the water. The elephants struggled in the uneven surface with deep pits. They realized that the Chalukyas had dug pits all over the river base.

Then the Cholas decided to stick to their plan of stopping the river flow with boulders and trees. The water flow slowed down and the river thinned out on the other side of the boulders. The boulders stood like a dam stopping the flow of the water.

The Chola forces could judge the terrain of the river base and cross over with little difficulty.

They crossed over and moved beyond the shores, there was no resistance whatsoever. But there were no people, the areas were deserted. During this uninterrupted march, suddenly one poisonous arrow hit Sundara Keralan, who was ahead of everyone.

He fell down. The people around him wanted to dip him into water but there was no pond around. They had to run to locate a pond. By the time they dipped him into water, he was dead. Sundara Keralan, the seventh son of Rajendra Chola, was no more.

When the news reached Rajendra Chola, who was coming along with Surya, he was devastated. He shouted, 'Sundara Keralan was a handsome boy, even when he was born. He was so adorable. How can I explain this to his mother?'

'Oh, Lord Shiva, why is it happening to me? I pulled him out of the Chera kingdom, where he was ruling. I killed him by calling him into this war. I killed him! I killed him! I do not want to move further, let me stop here.'

Araiyan Rajan, Surya and others tried to console their king. 'Your Majesty, you taught us that uncertainty is most certain in this world. You know this more than anyone else. Now we need you. You have to lead from the front now to destroy Jayasimha and his men. Please calm yourself down and get back to normalcy otherwise the enemy's objective of devastating your mental strength by this cowardly act will be achieved. Please Majesty, let us get ready for the Masangi onslaught now, more than any other time.'

Surya tried to console his king. It was a great loss to him as well, as he had lost his friend and batchmate.

After a while, everyone came back to their senses and cremated Sundara Keralan there. Then all of them moved fast towards the Masangi Fort, where Jayasimha was hiding with his men.

A gruesome attack followed.

52

Masungi Fort

The high fort walls were made of a natural rock formation. Not only was it of great height but also led to the lower walls of the fort. These were also made up of rocks, thereby providing a perfect defence against the use of elephants to tear the walls down.

It was surrounded by hills on three sides and there was a huge lake at the back. The fort was surrounded by deep moats which prevented the enemy from coming near the walls. But the unique feature was that the gate of the palace was really small.

Surya pointed out that the gates were kept small to allow the entry of one person only at a time and by the time the other one entered, the soldiers on either side of the gate could behead the entrant. The gate was kept small to arrest the speed of the entrants.

Araiyan Rajan was surveying the outer area of the fort for military formations. He divided his forces into three parts, one each for the north, the east and the west. Since the south was protected by water, he left it to Surya to handle with his regiment.

Surya presented his plan:

'Araiyan Rajan will attack the gates with elephants. We

should not wait till the morning. The people inside the fort would be waiting for us in the morning. The tall walls have to be conquered. The gates are small to filter the inflow and enable the beheading of incumbents by those inside guards. We have to set fire to the palace. The theme of this war is fire. Nothing should be left out.

'First, let us throw all the udumbus against the fort walls. The climbers have to tightly tie them to these monitor lizards and reach the top of the wall.

'Once they reach the wall, let them place the hooks on the wall and hang these huge nets to the hooks. Let them throw the other side of the net below. People from below can hang on to the nets through the entire wall. A group can climb up holding these nets. Once they all reach the top, they can get into the palace, pour oil on the gates and set them on fire. Then they can behead the in-house guards near the gates.

'In this melee, our commander can enter all the three sides with elephants breaking the walls. Let me take the two small boats and enter the rear side. Only twenty Oddha kingdom soldiers of my regiments will do for me.'

The plan was well executed. There was fire all over the gates, and the Chola forces entered the gates from all three sides. Once inside, fire arrows were thrown on all sides. The Chalukyas were surprised, woke up and ran in total confusion. They had thought that the Cholas would take more time to reach as they had dug pits in the Tungabhadra River. Their spy network had failed miserably.

Meanwhile, Surya went through the lakeside. He left two boats with the Oddas and swam below the water to enter the fort as there were no outer walls at the rear, since the lake itself was protecting the back.

As soon as he entered from the water, he did something. He looked for the food preparation unit. Food was being prepared for the night guards. He poured the poisonous liquid that he carried. Now, the entire food was poisoned.

Unaware of this, the food got distributed among the night guards. All of them were dead. Surya came out once he completed his mission and joined Araiyan Rajan at the front.

With the guards dead, the gates collapsed by fire, the entire Chola forces entered like a tsunami wave entering a sea town. The entire fort was now destroyed. All the valuables were taken by the Chola forces. The wealth looted from Vengi by the Chalukyas was hidden inside the walls. The loot was recaptured. But Jayasimha was able to escape. The spy forces found out that he had run away to Manyaketa, his western Chalukya capital. Even his commander was missing. He escaped but his whereabouts were not known. All his soldiers were imprisoned. The mission was accomplished as far as the fort demolition was concerned but the capture of Jayasimha remained an unfinished business yet again.

Rajendra Chola appreciated all his generals. Araiyan Rajan was busy arranging post-war changes. The wealth retrieved was to be transported to the Chola kingdom. He arranged all this. Rajendra Chola assembled all his generals.

'We have a message from Kashya Sharma from the north regional spy network controller. Vijayaditya, the puppet ruler installed in Vengi is now staying as a guest of Mahipala of Vangala Desha.'

'What? Mahipala is inviting troubles for his kingdom?' Surya shouted.

53

'Yes Surya, our enmity with Mahipala is confirmed. I was in two minds about whether to go that far. Now I am clear. We have two objectives for going after Mahipala. One, we have to capture the coveted regal jewels that have eluded us for generations. Two, Mahipala is supporting Jayasimha and that is why he is asserting himself to be a bigger power. We have to arrest Mahipala, eliminate Vijayaditya who has always been a threat to Raja Narendra in Vengi. Now Surya, what do you suggest?'

Araiyan Rajan was upset since Surya was young, and Araiyan Rajan was the commander-in-chief, high on seniority. Sensing this, Surya replied, 'Your Majesty, our commander-in-chief of the northern armed forces, Araiyan Rajan, can unveil his plan first. He is much more experienced than all of us.'

This statement cooled Araiyan Rajan down. He started unveiling his strategy: 'No Surya, we are all in this together. For us the Chola kingdom is first, everything else is next. My plan is: Let us split our forces into three. We have already left one lakh forces in Vengi. I will move with six lakh forces towards the north along with Paran Jothi. Your Majesty can go back to Vengi and stay at the banks of the Tungabhadra River with two lakh forces till we come back after conquering Mahipala. I know Your Majesty wants to come for the entire northern expedition, but your presence alone can control Jayasimha. We will come back to get him after we complete the northern expedition. Further, the coronation of Raja Narendra has to be arranged. We move north through the land route. In parallel, Arul Mozhi and Surya can move with one lakh forces via the eastern coast towards Vangala. Hope my plan meets your approval, Your Majesty.'

'I agree reluctantly. I will monitor from the Tungabhadra banks from this Masangi Fort. I will return only after all my forces have returned successfully.'

'You may factor this, Araiyan Rajan. You also do not go as one force. You divide your forces into two groups of three lakh each. One to be headed by you, another headed by Paran Jothi.

'Attack Manyaketta, destroy Jayasimha, then move to Oddha Desha, Kosala Desha, Dhadabukti, Daksnaladem and then Utraladem, Mahibalan's place. You go on landlocked route as two groups. Before you attack Mahipala, Surya will join you at sea, and Arul Mozhi will join you from the eastern coast routes. Mahipala has to be surrounded from all sides. He should be caught unawares.'

At that point, a messenger came in, and announced that Indra Dutta, the Oddha Desha king had come there to pay his respects to the Chola ruler. The Oddha king had a different story to tell the Chola ruler.

54

'Welcome, Your Majesty, the Oddha king. Your visit has surprised us. What would you like to tell us?'

'Your Majesty, the rising star of the Chola race, I have come here to understand your agenda in this region. Are you keen on conquering us and ruling us as a Chola province?'

'No, we conquer for a cause. We attacked Jayasimha because he played with our ally kingdom, Vengi. You all give your tacit approval to him. We want to conquer Mahipala, since he is holding our Chola pride—the regal jewels of the Pandyas—won by us but it came to Mahipala via Mahinda who we imprisoned. Your country is in the pathway towards Mahipala's Vangala. If you give us a passage then why should we fight against you? We do not encroach on another kingdom unless we have a reason to. Do you understand?'

'It is clear, Your Majesty. I am relieved. I do not lose my people's lives fighting other people's battles. Jayasimha was begging me to send him some of my soldiers. I told him that we would send him our troops. But we did not, as we do not want to antagonize you.

'But I have a problem. If I allow your military through my country, I will be attacked by Mahipala and his ally if they survive your attack. I am caught between two giants. Hence, I am a bit hesitant.'

Surya intervened, 'Sorry, Your Majesty for interrupting. I have an idea for the Oddha king. He can allow only 50,000 of our troops via his kingdom. They will pass through the coastal belt and climb northwards. I will take the sea route away from the Oddha lands. The bigger troops of Araiyan Rajan can take in the land route outside the border of Oddha Desha. The Oddha king can always say that he gave a passage to a small portion of the Chola troops who are coming to Vangala. He can say that he has agreed to this plan with the Cholas so that he can monitor their movements through his country to Mahipala. He can keep complete silence about the other two troops which were marching to Vangala Desha by different routes. He can claim ignorance in case he is asked about the other troops outside his kingdom.

'This will save his relationship with Mahipala. He can still be in his good books. But he has to agree to certain conditions of ours, if Your Majesty approves.

- He should pay annual tributes confirming his subordination to the Chola king.
- He should spare 3,000 of his elephants to us for our wars.
- He should depute some of his military commanders to us for guiding our way to Vangala Desha.
- He should keep all this information confidential and communicate with Vangala Desha, only on the movement of the small Chola forces through his kingdom.
- The Oddha king has to assist the Chola king to acquire some modern sailing vessels from traders navigating through the Oddha ports for our Chola navy.
- Any information on Jayasimha, Vijayaditya and Mahipala, should be shared with us confidentially.
- The Cholas will not damage his property and will be

> an ally forever and will come to his rescue in the event of any attacks.

Both rulers agreed to the proposals. The treaty was signed on the spot.

The Oddha Desha king sent twenty of his subcommanders to guide the marching Chola forces in three separate routes. Rajendra Chola stayed back with his two lakh forces ensuring that no one entered below the Tungabhadra River boundaries.

The three groups marched via separate routes towards the land of Mahipala.

55

Vangala Desha, Mahipala's Royal Darbar

The rulers, Ranasura of Dakshina Lada, Dharmapala of Dhadabukti and Govinda Chandra of Kosala were all assembled in the darbar of Mahipala.

'Welcome, we have to get united to fight the Cholas. It is survival for all of us. Rajendra Chola will not attack from the sea. He does not have enough ships. Further, the northeast monsoon has set in. Hence vessels cannot navigate towards our ports. Normally this is a time when the vessels move out from here using the northeast monsoon.'

Dharmapala of Dhandabukti chipped in.

'Rajendra Chola will come on a straight line upwards north. He will march towards Dakshina Lada through Dhandabukti. If he is stopped there, then Kosala Desha and Dakshina Lada will escape. Hence, all these countries will have to block Rajendra Chola at the entry point of Dhandabukti. The Oddha Desha king Indradutta is with them on the war. He preferred to permit the troops of Chola with the tacit agreement with us that he will regularly pass on information about the movement of the Chola forces to us. Let him not openly support us. His disguised neutral posture can give us intelligent inputs on the Cholas' movements.'

They all agreed. They also agreed to give valuables, horses

and elephants to Mahipala within seven days in return of his support. All of them knew Mahipala's support was required to defend against the Cholas. Meanwhile, the three groups of Cholas marched through different routes. Indradutta informed Mahipala that only a small force of 50,000 Cholas would cross through Oddha Desha towards Dhandabukti on their way to Vangala.

His generals guided the Chola forces separately on how to cross the marshy land and the Mahanadi River on their way towards Vangala (also known as Uthra Lada).

Surya bought two vessels at the Oddha port—an Arabian one and a Chinese one. Since the northeast monsoon was delayed, the wind direction was not hostile to his movement towards Vangala. He followed the current of the sea by locating the movements of tortoises and hence the movement in the sea was faster for him.

Before moving in the new sea vessel from the Oddha Desha's port, Surya got back to his vessel with enough drinking water, rice, dried fish and honey. Horses were carefully placed in the lower deck. Apart from this, camphor oil and cloth for placing on the edges of arrows were all adequately stacked.

Oddha Desha's generals were guiding Arul Mozhi moving through the eastern coast. They were crossing dense forests infested with poisonous insects and marshy lands. They crossed the Mahanadi River by placing wooden planks on top of the elephants standing in a row across the river. They also carried rope bridges to cross the marshy surface. The guidance of the Oddha Desha generals was very helpful to Arul Mozhi and his team.

The big forces with Araiyan Rajan moved in two groups on the land via eastern Kosala Desha. When he crossed each side of Kosala Desha, he understood their ruler Govinda Chandra was a weak personality. The ruler was a Brahmin, who wanted to keep off from wars. In fact without any resistance Araiyan Rajan entered Kosala Desha.

Govinda Chandra sent a secret message to Araiyan Rajan that the gold and horses were being moved to Mahipala as per their treaty. After agreeing to the treaty with Mahipala on the one hand, Govinda Chandra also informed him about the movement of valuables to Araiyan Rajan. He played a double game. He shifted his loyalty to the Cholas, once he saw their large forces entering his country. He was told of a small force coming via Oddha Desha.

Understanding the route of gold and horses to Mahipala, Araiyan Rajan captured them, and then sent empty pots along with useless sick horses to Mahipala. Once Mahipala received the useless consignment from the other rulers, he got wild. He did not know about the trick played by the Chola commander. He decided to teach them a lesson. He stopped sending any forces to their rescue. Thus the treaty signed by them turned out to be a futile one.

56

Surya entered Vangala from the sea. Meanwhile, Araiyan Rajan and Paran Jothi arrested the rulers of Kosala, Dhandabukti and Dakshina Lada.

Araiyan Rajan attacked Uthra Lada from the west. Arul Mozhi attacked with his forces from the south. Three-corner attacks were unleashed on Mahipala who was certainly not expecting it. All along he was informed of the small 50,000 soldiers crossing Oddha Desha. Mahipala tried to escape in the disguise of a common man, but he was arrested by the Chola forces who were supported by an excellent spy network system.

All these arrested rulers were made to bring the Ganga water in vessels by carrying it on their heads.

The Ganga water was taken in abundance in various vessels and the donkeys carried them towards Chola Desha. Abundant valuables won by the Cholas were also transported.

All of them were received by Rajendra Chola near the Tungabhadra River. He appreciated Araiyan Rajan, Arul Mozhi, Surya and all his forces. He rewarded them and also conferred prestigious titles on them.

He turned his attention to the rulers of the various kingdoms. He released them with a treaty agreed by them that they will pay annual tributes in exchange of accepting their subservience to the Chola kingdom. But he did not release Mahipala. He asked him, 'Tell me, where is Vijayaditya? And Narasimha, the general of Jayasimha, who took shelter with you?'

'They ran away, once your forces entered Vangala Desha. I do not know their whereabouts.'

'Tell me, where are the royal crown and the regal jewels of the Pandyas, deposited with you by Mahinda. You know Mahinda is in my prison for his entire lifetime. Do you want to be in one? Tell me the truth.'

'Your Majesty, please forgive me. As soon as you started marching towards the north, I got the message through Lankan traders that I had to pass them on for safe custody to Vijayathunga Varman, the king of Srivijaya in the far-east. Since these traders always transit from Lanka via our Vangala ports, it was easy for me to shift them.

'I never knew about your rights over these regal jewels. Since it came to me for safe custody as the Lankan king's jewels, I honoured his request, thinking that he was the owner of these regal jewels. I do not know about your rightful claim over these. I have not passed them on to deny you your rights. Please do not punish me for that. As far as Jayasimha and his general are concerned, I agree, I will cease my relationship with them. I guarantee you my kingdom will not do anything that damages the interests of your kingdom. Please release me. I agree to pay the annual tribute to your kingdom.'

Rajendra Chola was moved, so he released Mahipala upon signing a treaty.

Having completed the Ganga mission, the coronation of Raja Narendra as the Vengi king was done. Rajendra Chola decided to give his daughter Ammanga in marriage to the Vengi king, thereby cementing a strong relationship between the Chola and Vengi kingdoms.

Then he had a review meeting with his generals. 'What next?'

'Generals, do we go against the dacoit Mahmud of Ghazni, who robs the wealth of the northern kingdoms of our Bharat? Maybe our northern kings can defend themselves. I do not want to tame the robber Ghazni. We have a pressing obligation from the fareastern Srivijaya kingdom and the surrounding regions. Look at these reasons:

'First and foremost, we need to capture the royal crown and the regal jewels. We cannot move away from this objective.

'Our traders have been ill-treated, imprisoned, amputated by the Srivijaya king who is jealous of our growing trade with China.

'I have more compelling reasons to march to the southeast nations. The Sailendra dynasty had good relations with the Chola empire during the period of my father. My father encouraged Mara Vijayathunga Varman to build the Chudamani Vihara in Nagapattinam. I still continue to be friendly with Srivijaya. We had an active trade relationship with the eastern island. Moreover, the Srivijaya kingdom and our empires had been the intermediaries in the trade between China and the countries of the western world. Both Srivijaya and us had active dialogue sessions with the Chinese and sent diplomatic missions to China. The first mission to China from us reached that country a few years ago. But China told our diplomat that the Srivijaya kingdom misrepresented the information that the Cholas are subservient to Srivijaya. The commercial intercourse between us and the Chinese have been continuous and extensive. There arose trade disputes stemming from some attempts by Srivijaya to throw some obstacles between the flourishing trade between China and us. I need to the tame Srivijaya kingdom.

Piracy: The strategic position of Srivijaya and Khamboj

(modern-day Cambodia) as a midpoint in the trade route between Chinese and Arabian ports was crucial. We and the Arabs traded with the Chinese directly using Srivijaya as a port of call and a replenishment hub. Realizing their potential, the Srivijaya empire began to encourage piracy surrounding the area. The benefits were twofold, the loot from piracy was a good bounty and it ensured their sovereignty and cooperation from all the trading parties. Piracy also grew stronger due to a conflict of succession in Srivijaya, when two princes fought for the throne and in turn, relied on the loot from the piracy for their civil war. The menace of piracy reached unprecedented levels. Sea trade with China was virtually impossible without the loss of one-third of the convoy for every voyage. Even escorted convoys came under attacks, which became a new factor. Repeated diplomatic missions urged the Srivijaya empire to curb piracy with little effect. With the rise in piracy, and in the absence of the Chinese commodity, the Arabs, on whom we are dependent on horses for their cavalry corps began to demand high prices for their trade. This led to a slew of reduction in our army. The Chinese were equally infuriated by the menace of piracy, as they too were losing revenue. This has made the southeast expedition more important for me now.

'Also, we have a naval force established from my father's days. Now we have acquired many ships of various kinds with more than one lakh navy men.

'Therefore, we are launching our naval expedition to the far-eastern kingdoms. Understand?'

The guards looked at him.

Araiyan Rajan asked who was deputed for that expedition.

'Araiyan Rajan, you will guard the Tungabhadra River boundary with three lakh forces and assist Raja Narendra, the Vengi king and my son-in-law. I need peace in this region so that we can go all out for this naval expedition. I go far-east with Arul Mozhi and Bheema Sena, the east-wing sea commander.

'We move in a month or two.

'But before that I nominate Surya to go over there with Li Yuang, since he may need the support of Chinese language. Surya will evaluate the region, set our naval base before we reach, and he will ultimately give all the intelligence support for the sea expedition.

'Arul Mozhi will head the land-based expedition in and around Srivijaya. Bheema Sena will command the ships. I will head the expedition myself.'

'The dependence on Surya is growing,' murmured Araiyan Rajan.

Rajendra Chola overheard him.

'Araiyan Rajan, listen to this. Surya let me tell you openly that you will one day be jalathipathy of our entire Chola kingdom. You will see, he will prove me right soon.'

'Your Majesty, I am grateful for the confidence you have shown in me. Only with the guidance and well wishes of great commanders such as Araiyan Rajan and Bheema Sena, can I perform well,' Surya eased the situation a little.

He went on, 'Your Majesty, we need to have more fleets in our navy. We had to assemble them quickly.'

'Surya, we have our team under the disguise of the dacoits in and around Srivijaya. They robbed twenty vessels from the dacoits and continue to send us. We have assembled a fleet of five hundred vessels at Mullaitivu, our southern island. We have built five hundred vessels by using Arab and Chinese technical personnel in the shipbuilding yard over the past few years,' said Rajendra Chola.

'We already have about 250 vessels with us. You buy or rob from dacoits and assemble another 250 vessels in the next two months before we arrive. Thus we will have a fleet strength of about 1,500 sailing vessels in two months' time. We have more than three lakh army men ready to travel with elephants and horses anytime. In addition to these warships, we have—akramandhram (a vessel with the royal quarters), neela mandhram (a vessel with facilities for conducting courts and accommodation for the king's officers) and sarpa mugam (a smaller yacht used in river with a snake head). You take each one of these types of yachts along with a warship, as you are going on an intelligence gathering mission at first stage. What more do you want, Surya?'

'Amazing plan, Your Majesty. I will move in a week after attending the wedding of our princess to the Vengi king. Meanwhile one disturbing news has reached Vengi through the spy network. Narasimha; the general of defeated Jayasimha, the Chalukya king, has come to Vengi in disguise with a mission to kill Rajendra Chola. The terrorists decide their time and venue. In what form and when they come can not be predicted. This message comes from the headquarters of Thanjavur, from Krishna Raman. We cannot take this lightly,' Surya told Arul Mozhi.

Both decided to provide a close security cordon to their king till the wedding got over. They expected the attack could be during the wedding when the ruler's exposure to public would be very high.

The wedding day arrived. There was a grand function, marking the union of two kingdoms.

Surya and Arul Mozhi were alert looking for any potential

threats. During the evening function, a music concert was held in the open-air stadium as a part of celebrations. The Chola ruler was in the front seat closely guarded by Surya and Arul Mozhi.

Suddenly they saw an arrow, coated with poison flying from a flute. Ajili quickly flew in between the ruler and the arrow, which hit Ajili and it died on the spot. The security officials were quick to catch the flutist. He was none other than Narasimha. He was immediately jailed.

The wedding ended well. There was happiness all around.

But Surya lost his closest ally Ajili. Ajili's partner Gujili attached itself closely to Surya thereafter. Surya did not want to leave Gujili alone. Both of them soon started their challenging sea journey to the far-eastern kingdoms together.

PART VII

The Love That Blossomed

57

Surya took the three vessels—akramandhram, neela mandram and sarpa mugam. He made some amendments to Akramandhram on which he was sailing. Some of his horses, food articles and a few supporting deputy commanders occupied neela mandram. A few soldiers disguised as traders were sailing in sarpa mugam.

Li Yuang acquainted himself with the region's history, topography, culture and so on.

'Li Yuang, you are a champion of this region, even though you have lived most of your life in our Chola kingdom. Some call it Svarna Bhoomi, some Srivijaya, what is this place all about?'

'Surya, you have started your intelligence gathering right on our sea travel. It is an archipelago, comprising many islands: Svarna Island (modern-day Sumatra), Savaga Island (modern-day Java), Kadaram (modern Kedah in Malaysia), Pali and so on.

'Gold is available on these islands. That is why the Greeks called it Svarna Island or Svarna Bhoomi. The sand has gold particles mixed in it. The terrain is land-locked with the Bharat continent but split by sea below Kadaram into many islands—Svarna, Savaga and Pali Islands and so on.

'Srivijaya city was established on the banks of the Musi River. The port of Srivijaya served as an important port for valuable commodities from the region—rice, cotton, indigo and silver from Java; resin, camphor, ivory and rhinos' tusks from Sumatra; rare timber, rare animals, iron and sandalwood from Kadaram are all traded from this region. Chinese sell porcelain silk here while they buy spices, perfumes from the Cheras and horses from the Arabs.

'Traders from the Chola kingdom, Arab Peninsula and China are all attracted to this region of transhipment trade.

'Srivijaya controls Keda, Lemuri Desh, Jambu, Pannai (Panai) and Lanka Suka. They control two major check points—Malacca and Sunda straits. The Strait of Malacca is controlled from Kadaram and Pannai. Malayu and Srivijaya ports control Sunda strait. They practised naval trade monopoly that forced any trade vessel that passed through their waters to call on their ports or otherwise being plundered. Srivijaya also has rivalries with neighbouring Savaga Island, Kamboja (modern-day Cambodia) and Champa. They gave trade links with Mahipala of Vangala Desha as well as with the Islamic caliphate in the Middle East.

'But Srivijaya has its quota of rivalries. They passed inaccurate information about our Chola kingdom to the Song dynasty which rules China. When we directly sent our diplomatic mission, we came to know that Srivijaya has misrepresented the information that the Chola kingdom is a province of theirs. In order to gain a higher status for them, they seem to have done that. This led to limited direct access for our traders to the Chinese markets. We had to go through the transhipment centre, Srivijaya. We were thought to be a vassal state of Srivijaya by the Chinese dynasty. This has completely irritated our ruler. Not only that, our traders are tortured, imprisoned and forced to pay higher taxes and the pirates with the tacit approval from the Srivijaya kingdom looted our traders. All this because of their assumption that the Cholas cannot come here to attack. While they were diplomatic with the Chinese because they feared that they could easily access their terrain and attack.'

'Fantastic description, Li Yuang. Do they have a cordial relationship with Kamboja?' Surya intervened. 'Suryavarman of Kamboja requested aid from our ruler Rajendra Chola against the Tambralinga kingdom (modern-day—southern Thailand/Malay peninsula).

'After learning about Suryavarman's alliance with our ruler, Tambralinga requested aid from Srivijaya King Vijayathunga Varman. They readily agreed since they strongly believe that Rajendra Chola cannot come this far to attack them. The latest civil war in this region is hotting up as a religious war between the Shaivites (Cholas and Kambojas) and Buddhists (Tambralinga and Srivijaya).'

Srivijaya Empire in the 10th and 11th Centuries

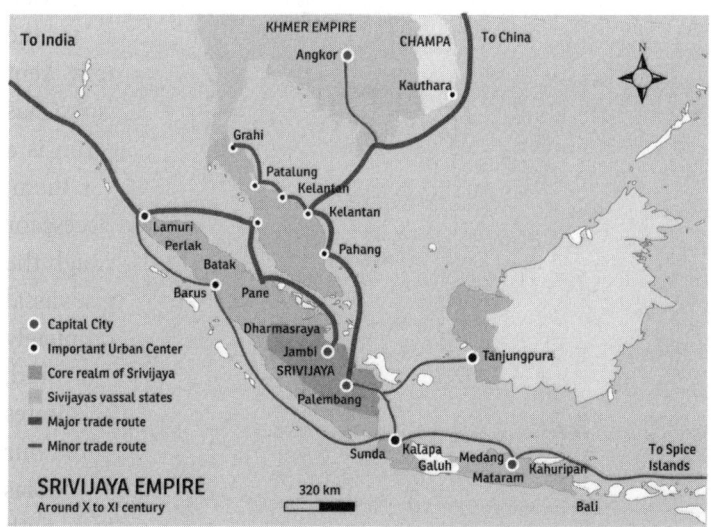

As the vessel continued to sail towards Srivijaya, both friends kept on discussing about it.

Maximum Extent of Srivijaya Empire around 8th Century

The Srivijayan Expedition and Rajendra Chola

58

Lemuri Desh (modern-day northern Sumatra, Indonesia)

The sailing vessels of Surya landed in the port of Lemuri. It was located in the Aceh province near Banda Aceh, on the northern tip of the Srivijaya kingdom.

The island was washed by two seas, Harkand and that of Salahit. The island produced bamboo and Brazil wood, the roots of which were used as antidotes for deadly poisons. There were also gold and camphor mines. The island face many storms and earthquakes.

As Lemuri was a hot country, people went about naked. All women were shared, that is, no one who anyone's wife. There aboriginals were cannibals, who purchased children from merchants to slaughter them.

It was a hot day, and it looked as if Lemur extended its head outside the sea, welcoming Surya and his team. There was a huge mountain in the backdrop.

With minerals mixed with it, the sand looked reddish. At a distance, there were signs of volcanoes which kept showing tongues of fire off and on.

Not far off, a fort with well laid-out watchtowers was guarding the city. The houses were made of bamboos. Those houses were located in groups as if there were separate streets.

'Li Yuang, why are these streets separated here?'

'Surya, people from different places—Bharat Varsha, Arabia, Africa and Bali Islands all come here for trade or sea-related activities. Each of the nationalities lives as a colony. There is also a Tamil colony comprising people from the Chola and Pandya kingdoms. They generally coexist peacefully focusing on their professions.

'Please look at the grand-looking houses. They are transit houses of pirates. The Srivijaya king has given tacit approval to them to loot our ships. They pay one-third of the looted wealth to the ruler's representatives here.'

'Where do the cannibals live?'

'They live in the mountains but occasionally visit the port town and these pirates share some of their loot with them too. Sometimes the pirates share the captured children and women with the cannibals. The cannibals give nara bali (human as a sacrifice to God) of children, and rape the women.

'When the pirates attack the town, the ruler cannot do anything. The ruler can only get support from the headquarters of the Srivijaya kingdom after a few days.

'Therefore the rulers have to keep all the stakeholders—aboriginals, different trade groups and the pirates happy at all times.'

'Oh my God, the kingdom runs in partnership with the pirates? Atrocious! That is why we are here to break the backbone of this unholy alliance that disturbs our trade with China. Understand Li Yuang? Who are the rulers here? Li Yuang, any idea?'

'Here, one of the pirates called Kumara Bahu from the Lankan kingdom is the ruler's representative. He supports the young Princess Luli. It is a Chinese name that means dewy jasmine. I do not know why they used a Chinese name for her. Once we start interacting with the people, we will know.'

'Li Yuang, we may start our operations from here at Lemuri. We may set up our base here for intelligence operations. We need a clear war strategy, three months before our ruler Rajendra Chola heads here, with his fleet towards Srivijaya. Stay alert, stay calm. Keep your ears and eyes open. Ask our sailors and support staff to get into the town, relax and come back on the siren sound mimicking a tiger's roar from the vessels. Let all the small boats inside our vessels be taken out and placed outside. Let the horses come out with our men and breathe the land air. Let them also stretch their legs. We have to move through the trade and customs officials. Let me declare some spices to the customs which I am anyway going to sell here for raising money for our day-to-day activities. Let others move without any custom declaration. Let them not carry anything inside so that they can have free access.'

All of them started moving into the shores not knowing what was waiting for them in the town.

59

'What have you to declare for our customs?' the customs officer asked Surya.

The others passed ahead of him since they had nothing to declare.

Surya replied, 'Spices from the land of Cheras'. The answer was crisp as he did not believe in giving too many details for the officials.

'What about the ring with the seal of a tiger embossed on it?' the custom officer asked.

'That is my personal possession, I will take it back with me. It is not for trade.'

When he was answering, two guards speaking some other language alien to him frisked him away. His support staff and Li Yuang were helplessly watching this. Surya knew that Li Yuang would manage the requirements of his staff, but he did not know what mistake he had made to warrant an arrest in this alien country.

After a few nazhigas (one nazhiga equals to twenty-four minutes) he was inside the fort jail.

'What did I do to land in this jail?' Surya asked helplessly shouting.

'You will soon get the answer from our commander, Kumara Bahu,' came the reply from the jailer.

After a while, he was taken to the fort court hall. A reasonably well-built man, aged around fifty, was sitting on an ornamented chair. *The ornaments of the chair might have been a part of the loot from our Chola traders*, Surya could not stop thinking about the miseries these pirates or their partners in crime, the rulers of the Srivijaya kingdom, inflicted on the peace-loving Chola traders.

Surya looked at this commander. *He seems to be from the Chera or Chola or Pandya kingdom in Lanka, generations*, he thought. He was dark-skinned, well-built with streaks of silver hair on his head. He had a poker face.

'Welcome, representative of Rajendra Chola...'

Surya was stunned. *How did he know? Do they also have a spy network far beyond the seas?*

'No, I am a regular peace-loving trader from the land of the Cholas. I am here to sell my spices and in turn take back perfumes and camphor to our country. Why am I arrested and harassed like this?'

'Yes, you are one. Your ring carries the raja mudra of Rajendra Chola. These are carried only by men who have direct access to the king. They are a part of his team and are not traders. You have camouflaged your identity therefore you are a criminal in my eyes,' the commander retorted.

At that point a strange thing happened, as the area got brightened.

60

'What is it Commander Uncle?' a pleasant female voice asked. She looked almost like an angel.

Surya could not take his eyes off of her. She had very graceful movements. He had never seen such a beauty. She was pale, with small but penetrative eyes. *She had Chinese features but her long and dense black hair added the touches of a Dravidian maiden*, Surya thought.

Surya was mesmerized by her dense black eyebrows, lovely cheeks and beautiful dimples.

Slowly, he was able to bring himself back to reality. At that moment, both of them looked at each other.

He could guess she was Luli.

Luli looked at Surya, surveyed him from head to toe. He looked like an ordinary twenty-five-year-old man, but his eyes showed a maturity much beyond his age. The scars on his face added majesty to his looks. The dense black hair falling on his strong broad shoulders, the broad forehead, a brownish face with sharp features confirmed his warrior traits.

He must be a great warrior. He must have seen many victorious wars at a young age, Luli thought.

Surya's jewel-studded short sword and golden-bordered; clothes indicated his royal connections. Above all, he looked firm and far-sighted.

She finally spoke, 'Commander Uncle, who is he? Why have you arrested him?'

'He has hidden his real identity. He looks like a warrior attached to the royal command force of Rajendra Chola. He seems to have direct access to his ruler. Let me imprison him.'

'Will it not invite the wrath of the Chola ruler? What would my father Vijayathunga Varman of Srivijaya think about this? Have you thought about this, Commander Uncle?'

'Sure, Luli, first of all, the Chola ruler cannot come this far. As far as our king is concerned, he will be happy to have a catch. He may ask us to extract more information from this man, who calls himself Surya. He appears to be an influential royal commander of the Cholas.'

As Surya was listening to these conversations, he knew that he had to stay in the jail for now. But one thing that struck him was that there was an element of sadness in the eyes of the beautiful princess.

However, an opportunity to move out of the jail came soon.

61

In the jail, Surya came to know that Princess Luli was born to an unwed mother and the current Srivijaya king. Her mother was promised once that she would become the queen. Unfortunately, before her marriage, she died in an accident, within one month after delivering Luli.

Since the king felt guilty that he could not marry her on time before the baby was born, he made his daughter the princess of this place under the guidance of Kumara Bahu, his trusted lieutenant.

The king later married the present queen, and had two daughters and a son with her. Surya also came to know that Kumara Bahu hailed from the Chola kingdom but descended from the Lankan kingdom. He was operating as a pirate in this region and the Srivijaya king patronized pirates. Kumara Bahu eventually became close to the king and now he is supporting the princess as her commander uncle.

But now they were facing a serious problem. On the previous night, a group of hostile pirates landed here. Their head Gomango, a Mongolian pirate, accidentally saw Princess Luli swimming in the river and was smitten by her. He now wants her to sleep with him and for the rest of the next ten days with his co-pirates, one after the other.

When Kumara Bahu rushed to the spot and tried to save her, Gomango shouted at him, 'You are heading the land of cannibals where there is free sex. Anyone can have sex with anyone of their choice.'

He was waiting for the princess to give him company that night. Sending a message to the Srivijaya king and getting additional support would take time, but the forces were so small here, they needed the support of other pirates to counter Gomango. But his very name made the other pirates scared and no one wanted to come to the rescue of the princess.

When Surya learnt about the crisis, he called in the jailer.

'Please take me to the commander and princess. I can save them.'

The jailer did not take him seriously at all. But Surya kept on insisting and refused to take lunch and resisted taking water as well.

Finally, the jailer took Surya to the commander and Luli. Surya told them, 'I will save the princess from this situation.'

When he unveiled his plan, the commander and the princess were both stunned.

62

Gomango should be told that he could have Princess Luli for that night, only when he defeats Surya, the representative of Lemuri town in a water boxing challenge. Being a sea city, underwater boxing was a convention when any fight arose regarding the right over a girl.

Initially, the commander thought that Gomango was a gigantic figure who would overthrow Surya in seconds. But Surya was pestering them to take this chance as they had nothing to lose and no other options in their hands. Surya said he would go back to his ship and come back to the site where the water boxing was arranged. Meanwhile, the commander had to talk to Gomango and arrange for the contest.

The fight was arranged. Surya looked at Gomango: a towering man with a bulky head, bulging eyes and a long moustache. He looked rather scary.

Gomango asked, 'Is this worthless idiot going to fight me in water boxing?'

'Yes, Your Excellency, let us not waste time in talking. Let us go underwater and fight.'

A huge crowd had gathered.

Both went under the water. Surya deliberately dodged Gomango underwater for more than three nazhigas. Gomango could not hold his breath and was struggling. Soon Surya gave a hard kick and Gomango had to come out to stay alive.

During the fight, Kumara Bahu did not fail to notice the

big fish-shaped birthmark on the chest of Surya. It rang a bell in his head.

Meanwhile, Surya was announced as the winner. Luli was very happy. But Gomango roared, 'You cannibals, you have cheated me. I will destroy this whole island. Let me unleash fire arrows on this island from the ships. Go and get burnt.'

He then ordered his ten ships to surround the island and throw fire arrows on the bamboo structures.

But to his surprise, all his ships were sinking in the sea. What happened?

Gomango could not believe his eyes.

63

Surya explained…

Surya released twenty boats from his ship. All those boats had sharp thick iron rods fixed at their bottoms which could be extended or folded. Once the rods were extended they hit the bottom of each of the ten pirate vessels with force.

The sharp rods created deep holes in each of these vessels. Sea water was seeping in quickly, while their crew was watching the contest on the shore. As the vessels were left unattended, the sea water flooded these vessels.

Gomango and his men surrendered to Surya, accepting him as their leader. Kumara Bahu and Luli were extremely happy. A grand dinner was hosted honouring Surya and his men.

The next morning, Commander Kumara Bahu spoke to Princess Luli.

'Princess, our Srivijaya king came to know of the developments here. He also came to know that Surya is one of the greatest warriors of the Chola kingdom. It seems he won many wars for his king Rajendra Chola. If he marries you, the whole Srivijaya kingdom will be benefitted. He wants you to marry him.'

'What! He wants me to seduce Surya? Or does he think Surya's loyalty to his Chola kingdom is that of a fragile one?'

'I can understand the human psyche to a certain extent, Luli. Only because he was attracted to you, he volunteered to take on Gomango. I also know that you love Surya. I could see the love in your eyes when you saw him the first time. He will eventually have to decide in favour of love. Once both of you are in a relationship, our king wants to offer your hand and the Lemuri Island to him, provided he switches his loyalty. He will not want to lose you. Hence, he will eventually agree to this proposal. It is all in your hands. Seduce him in such a way that he cannot move away from you. Do you understand?'

Luli wanted to reflect on the offer. She preferred to swim naked which gave her the feeling of being aligned with nature. She got this habit by seeing the cannibal girls who loved free mixing with nature.

After a while, she got back to the shore to put her clothes on. She was shocked to see Surya who was watching her. She thought, *When did he get here?*

But Surya was in a state of trance. He could not control his emotions. He carried her and took her to a bamboo house on the riverbank. The next hour witnessed a great union. Like a river joining the sea with all forces, Surya and Luli the two souls became one, unmindful of their surroundings.

When they come back to their senses, Luli was shy. She took her clothes from where she had left them and gave a tight kiss to Surya. She then walked back to her fort.

Surya kept on looking at her until she disappeared.

The next morning turned him into a totally different man, as many events started unfolding quickly.

64

A few days later…

Kumara Bahu went to see Surya in his akramandhram. Surya took him around his ship and showed him all the aspects of the modifications he made in the ship.

'The ships of China are bulkier. They sink the opponent's ship just by collision. Due to the weight, the collision will cause damage to the opponent's ships. Our Chola vessels are lightweight, made out of wood.'

He pulled a lever, then many iron rods folded up as if they were implicitly obeying his command. 'The innumerable sharp rods at the bottom will pierce holes into the opponent's ships, if we collide our ship with them. That is how we sink the ships of our opponents.

'We can also arrange our ship to quickly go low in height by dipping its bottom more into the sea at the turn of this other lever. When the opponent attacks with fire arrows we can temporarily go deeper into the sea, reduce our height suddenly and all the fire arrows shot on our ships will fall into the sea, not on our ships.

'We have two invisible wings to our ship. We can open the wings on either side, thereby creating a new base floor for our soldiers to throw their arrows and spears. Since it is an extended wing suddenly appearing near the ships of the opponent, they will be surprised by the sudden attacks'.

Kumara Bahu was speechless. 'We have more, there were

three levels in the ship. At each level there are a series of holes going throughout the circumference of the ship. Normally it is closed. But at the click of this lever, all holes will get open. One set of holes have fire arrows from behind them, another set has poison-tipped arrows and the last one has spears. From the outside, enemy cannot see these weapons or holes through which they were pointing out.'

'Extraordinary, Surya, your vessel is no wonder named Samudra Raja,' said Kumara Bahu. After taking a round, they sat in his royal chamber for lunch. After the lunch was served, Kumara Bahu said.

'I want to ask you a personal question: Who are your parents? Where do they live?'

'It is a long story. I was born to an unwed mother, my father ditched her. It seems he ditched her and ran away with the treasures of the Chola king. She did not know where he ran away. But she branded him a traitor. She also treated me as a traitor's son born with all his sins. Hence, she refused to even touch me, when I was born. I could not feel my mother's warmth. I don't even know who my father is,' his voice was choking.

'Relax, Surya, then what happened?'

'My mother's jailer gave me to his brother and their family brought me up. His wife breastfed me along with her newborn son. They formally adopted me. I have come this far due to their support. Then destiny took me to the ruler. Life has changed after that. It is a long story.'

Surya was wiping his tears.

Kumara Bahu bid goodbye and departed.

The next day brought the major turning point in the life of Surya.

65

Kumara Bahu returned with a heavy heart. Something was really troubling him. 'What is bothering you, Commander Uncle?'

He then explained all the incidents that Surya had narrated to him.

'Luli, it is time you acted. We need to convert his loyalty towards our Srivijaya kingdom. The king said he will arrange for the marriage, make him the king of Lemuri Island but on the condition that he switches his loyalty. Love or loyalty to the Cholas? He has to decide fast. Go and check, as we have to go ahead with the marriage plans.'

Luli promised to raise the subject with Surya and went to his royal yacht. 'Surya, I have come here to fix our wedding date. My father had agreed to our marriage. He has even decided to make you the king of Lemuri, but on one condition. You should become an ally of Srivijaya severing your Chola connections.'

'What! Severing Chola connections? Even in my dreams it cannot happen. My blood is Chola blood. I do not know my father. I was born to an unwed mother. Being a Chola is my only identity.

'For heaven's sake, do not ditch me, Surya. Your child is growing within me. I was also born to an unwed mother. I was not given the chance to live in the palace of my father, who is living with his queen and other daughters from the queen. I have been isolated by my father by being appointed as a princess on this far-off island. Let our child also not be given birth by an unwed mother. Let that stigma be over. Marry me. Let your loyalty for the country not kill our love and create a bastard.'

She cried uncontrollably. Surya took her in his arms, kissed her warmly and said, 'Luli, I am not a heartless person. I will not decide anything that is detrimental to your interests. I promise you. I am now confused, so give me a few days. Let me take the right decision.'

With these words, Surya consoled her. He did not want her to go alone. He came all the way and dropped her back to the fort. Luli narrated the happenings to Kumara Bahu who promised her he would do his best to convince Surya. He went ahead and made a startling revelation that shook Surya.

66

Kumara Bahu met Surya the next day. He told him he needed to talk to him.

'Surya, your mother called your father a traitor. Do you know who is that traitor? It is none other than me.'

'What! Are you my biological father? Are you a Chola traitor? You work for our enemy kingdom. I am ashamed to hear this. My god, did I live this long to learn about this treacherous act of my father?'

'Surya. Listen to me first then take a call. I was the most loyal soldier of the Cholas in the war, the former ruler of the Chola kingdom, Raja Raja Chola waged against the Lanka kingdom. But your mother used to say: "Amongst the lakhs of Chola soldiers you were also one. In your family all the earlier generations died in wars. In front of your eyes you lost both your brothers at the tender age of eighteen. They did not even have a proper life. There are too many young widows in your family. Why should you lose your people for a king whose clan is growing? They enjoy the fruits of the labour over all your dead bodies?"

'She had not forgotten the rape attempts of Chola soldiers on her. She was also upset that Lankan King Mahipala was jailed and stationed at your kingdom as a prisoner. But I always countered her, "Do not poison my mind, darling, I am an incorrigible emotional idiot, but I breathe for my Chola kingdom."

'She used to make fun of me. Your mother is distantly related to King Mahinda, who is in the custody of your country. I saved her from the Chola soldiers who were trying to rape her after the last Lanka war. I saved her by saying she is my wife and made her stay with me. Eventually, we got emotionally involved. When she got pregnant with you we agreed to solemnize our marriage at Rameswaram temple later.

'Meanwhile, I was assigned the task of accompanying one of the many vessels carrying our captured wealth from Lanka to the Chola kingdom. Since I promised your mother to solemnize the marriage in Rameswaram, I took her with me.

'At that point, some Srivijaya and Lankans, surrounded our ship. I realized that allowing their leader near the Chola kingdom would one day create a huge problem for the Chola throne. Already the country faced a near civil war before our former ruler Raja Raja came to power. I did not want another challenge to our Chola monarchy. So I decided to surrender and go with them so that I can kill that person, the threat to our monarchy. Even though I could have defeated them, I surrendered to them. I had no time to inform your mother. Further, I did not want to reveal the secret to anyone, till I had eliminated the threat to our kingdom.

'As I left with them, your mother said she would wait for me at Rameswaram and stayed back in the deserted vessel.

'Later I came to know from my sources that she accused me of being a traitor, and tried to earn sympathy of the Chola soldiers who rescued her along with this abandoned vessel. But they did not listen to her story, and instead jailed her.

'The jail life and separation from me slowly drove her mad. She started believing that I ditched her. Her hatred was first towards me, later towards you. I kept getting information from Srivijaya traders till she was in jail. I also came to know of your big fish-like birthmark. The moment I saw it on your chest when you were fighting with Gomango, I sensed you could be my son. Now it has turned out to be true. Come on my son, let me embrace you and feel your warmth.'

'Please keep your distance. You may articulate a hundred reasons to justify your action against our kingdom. You may be my biological father, but I have a godfather, and where I am today is because him. That is our ruler Rajendra Chola.'

Every word came out like a fast-moving arrow with speed and full conviction.

'Surya, I had an important agenda. I had to remove an important threat to our Chola kingdom—a person who could have overthown the ruler and create a civil war. That person had to be removed away from the proximity of Chola kingdom. That is the main reason I agreed to move away with him as well as the looted wealth. I cannot disclose who he is. If I do it, there will be a serious trouble to our Chola monarchy. I will tell this only after I eliminate that person. He is still at large, escaped from me and his whereabouts is not yet known to me. He must be somewhere here in this region. I am still looking for him. Hence, please do not pressurize me about that episode. Trust me, it had to be done for the benefit of the Chola kingdom. But leave that aside. Do you want to create another child born to an unwed mother like our family tradition?' asked Kumara Bahu.

'That is the only thing that is making me rethink,' Surya expressed his hesitation.

'Good, let me give you a suggestion. Agree to the condition of our Srivijaya kingdom, marry Luli, become the king of Lemuri. Once you become the king of Lemuri, you can be a bridge between Chola and Srivijaya.'

These last words made Surya agree to the condition, as he firmly believed he could unite both these kingdoms.'

The wedding was celebrated in a grand manner. When the news hit the shores of the Chola kingdom it created strong vibrations beyond Surya's expectations.

PART VIII

The Srivijaya Expedition

67

The three vessels of Surya were withdrawn immediately from Lemuri under the captaincy of Li Yuang. Those vessels and the Chola men minus Surya moved to Nakkavaram (Nicobar Islands), the new naval base of the Cholas.

Surya was extremely upset as Li Yuang departed without exchanging a word with him. But he re-established his connectivity with Rajendra Chola by exchanging messages through some trusted Chola traders who ran swift boats with valuables. He explained to the Chola ruler that he would try to bring the Srivijaya king close to the Chola kingdom. He will try to re-establish the same closeness that both kingdoms enjoyed during the rule of Raja Raja Chola.

He lived happily with Luli. The Srivijaya king was also happy that Surya would protect Srivijaya from any enmity that arose from the Cholas.

Luli was at her father's palace in Srivijaya kingdom, as she was due for her delivery. Surya was consistently giving information about the Cholas' engagement with the Srivijaya kingdom. He also tried to mediate in any Chola traders' disputes.

The Srivijaya king took a review of their military placements in the region. His commander-in-chief Baladeva explained to him how he handled his military and navy.

'Your Majesty, if at all we have problems, we will have it from Suryavarman of Kamboja who tried to attack the

Buddhist kingdom Tamralinga, our neighbour. They have asked for our support, we being Buddhist. Suryavarman has asked for Rajendra Chola's support.'

'Will the Cholas come this far, Surya?'

'No, I do not think that the Cholas have such a big naval power to come this far. They are new to the terrain. They will try to flex their muscles. If some vessels of the Cholas entered this water, many pirates stationed by us in this region will overpower them. But if the Cholas' vessels come as a part of the larger fleet, the pirates will not be able to handle them. We have to engage our navy.'

'Right Surya, if such a situation arises, how do we handle the Chola fleet?' Vijayathunga Varman asked.

'To sail from Dakshin Bharat, the vessels will first sail to Lemuri where I am placed. Hence, they will not come without informing me. The other option is that they may go to Kedah in Malay Peninsula before entering the Strait of Malacca in the north.

'If at all they come, they come to the northern strait, that is, Malacca Strait.

'Even if they come to the Strait of Malacca, your forces can stop them at the north prohibiting their entry into the southern straits of Sunda. If they come with their fleet up to the Strait of Malacca, I will be neutral and will not fight them. Your Majesty, I can give guidelines to your commander Baladeva in the background.'

Baladeva added, 'Your Majesty, we will keep our entire fleet of navy at Kedha and the surrounding areas at the northwest. We can also keep our land army at the northern bases such as Takkolam, Kedha and Lemur. The Cholas cannot come this far. Even if they send any fleet, they can come via the Strait of Malacca. By stationing our army at our northern bases, we will easily overpower them.

'We can keep a lean army strength at Srivijaya, where you are sitting comfortably with no threats whatsoever.'

The Srivijaya king was happy with his defence preparedness. The events that happened over the next few days were totally unexpected.

68

Rajendra Chola was getting ready to move to the Srivijaya kingdom. He started with a fleet of five hundred ships of various types.

Horses, elephants, food articles, clean water, camphor oil, poisoned arrows, depoisoning powders, spears were all loaded in different ships.

Five hundred persons per ship were loaded and a total of 2,00,500 army men were moving. It was a massive fleet engagement. The soldiers included both land and navy forces.

Surya Varman of Kamboja agreed to supplement the forces as and when required, he also agreed to supply fire arrows to the Cholas. The Chola forces were trained to counter fire arrows. They were also trained to identify landmines in the form of false floors concealing the deep pits. When there were road blocks in the form of fallen trees, the land forces were told how to clear them quickly.

Their vessels knew how to capture water currents, how to catch the right direction of winds, as these were clearly taught by the Chola Navy School. While the Cholas were moving with full force, the Srivijaya king was oblivious to these developments. He stuck to his plan of strengthening his northern bases at the Strait of Malacca.

He happily settled in Srivijaya city in his fort with no worries of Chola trouble.

Srivijaya was calm as the hectic army activity was centred

in the northern parts. Suddenly one night via the Strait of Sunda, the Chola fleet entered the fort via the Musi River. The city was plundered.

Srivijaya was unprepared for this surprise attack of the Cholas. They never expected the Cholas to reach the southern Strait of Sunda least of all their capital city.

The Chola navy was split into small groups and hit the city's north and south at the same time while the forces in Srivijaya were ransacking the capital city.

Pannai, Malayur, Mayirudingam, Lankasoka, Mapplam, Thalaikolam and Nakkavaram (Nicobar Islands) were all attacked at the same time. Taking advantage of the southwest monsoon, the Cholas prevented Srivijaya from preparing defences. Now only Kadaram was left. That required full force since the entire navy of Srivijaya was guarding Kadaram.

Meanwhile, Srivijaya was plundered—the king, queen and their daughter Ulang Kiu (Ulaga Nayaki) were all imprisoned.

The vidhyadhara-torana (jewelled arch) and the gate adorned with great splendour were plundered. The torana was hanging from the ceiling of the palace near the gate. It was studded with diamonds and pearls. It was guarded by chariots. The jewelled gate was another marvel. Pearls were hanging all over it. When the main gate was opened, the sounds were like that of the bells. Within the gate there were a number of small gates ornamented with glittering jewels. From one of the secret boxes of the gate, Surya located the royal crown, the mythical aaram and the precious pearls that the Pandyas had left with Mahinda. The Chola prestige had been restored. The treasure that the Cholas were looking for over the generations was finally captured. It was a glorious moment. Surya came running with those treasures and placed them at the feet of

Rajendra Chola.

'Well done, Surya,' Rajendra Chola patted Surya on his back.

The imprisoned Srivijaya king was perplexed.

'How come Surya, you are in the camp of the Cholas? You ditched me.'

Then Surya unveiled the secrets.

69

'Your Majesty, I genuinely love your daughter, but I cannot be disloyal to my beloved Chola kingdom. I made you trust me by supplying credible inputs on the Chola movements. I completely kept you in dark about the Chola plan of direct entry into the Sunda Strait.

'I only advised them to take that surprise route while I made you all believe that if at all they come, they will only come from the northern Strait of Malacca. All of you have been deliberately misled. It was me who advised the Cholas to split into groups and attack all the ports at the same time, that too in the night when your team was unprepared.

'The fact that a large fleet of five hundred ships were led by Rajendra Chola, was not known to any of your sources. We made you all believe that the Cholas will not come here for a direct attack.

'This trip enabled me to locate my father. He was none other than Kumara Bahu. We have lost him in this war. He died after being hit by a fire arrow. He deliberately made you all believe that he was a traitor to the Chola kingdom. He was planted by our Chola ruler long ago. He concealed his identity as a pirate and entered the Srivijaya kingdom.

'He was giving credible inputs about your kingdom to the Cholas through the Chola traders. As a pirate, he conquered many vessels and developed a secret naval base for the Cholas at Nakkavaram. After I came, I used the team of Gomango and company and conquered many of your vessels. We have added five hundred vessels to our naval base. With five hundred vessels which came with our ruler Rajendra Chola, we have assembled a total of thousand vessels, a strength which this region never witnessed in any naval attack. It is an unbeatable strength by any standards.

'We also made sure that the Chola ships were sailing in small groups on the high seas so that the naval expedition of the Chola army could not be guessed by your spies. No one knew that Rajendra Chola himself was leading this expedition. On top of it, I also continued to mislead you with wrong information. Hence your people could not guess anything about our attacks.

'What about Luli? Was she a part of this?' the Srivijaya king asked.

'Ask Luli herself,' Surya replied.

Luli stepped in. 'Till I came to Srivijaya city, I was loyal to you, my father. But when I was here, I heard you talking to your queen. You told her that you are using me as a sacrificial lamb. By using me you said you will win the loyalty of Surya. You also mentioned that once you neutralized the Cholas, you will drive Surya and me out of Lemuri and give it back to your daughters. On hearing this, I was very upset. I felt isolated. Surya consoled me and brought me back to normalcy. I shifted my loyalty to the Chola ruler after this episode.'

'Surya, what next?' Rajendra Chola asked him.

'Kadaram remains unconquered. Since it is guarded by the naval forces of Srivijaya we need to attack this way.

'Our navy forces will go in two groups of five hundred fleets each and attack them from the south and the west. Our land forces will go through the land route and attack from the east. Our ally Surya Varman of Kamboja will attack from the north. Kadaram will fall in one day, as it cannot withstand this multi-cornered attack.'

Surya's brilliant plan was executed to perfection.

Kadaram was also conquered.

Srivijaya Thungavarman agreed to pay annual tributes and become subservient to the Chola kingdom. He also agreed to marry his daughter Ulang Kiu to Rajendra Chola. But his second daughter Tunga Devi escaped to Savaga kingdom and married King Arilangaa, hitherto an arch-rival of Vijayathanga Varman. Rajendra Chola appointed Li Yuang as his representative in Srivijaya.

With the mission accomplished, Rajendra Chola sailed back to his kingdom along with his wife, Surya and his pregnant wife and a larger fleet of the Cholas.

The Chola traders returned to smoothen the trade. Vijayathanga Varman, the Srivijaya king became an ally of the Cholas.

PART IX

Return to the Capital

70

As the Chola fleet was nearing the port of Nagapattinam, Rajendra Chola gave awards to many commanders, deputy commanders, deputy admirals and foot soldiers on board.

The treasures they got from Srivijaya were distributed amongst the Chola soldiers. Many of the soldiers were elevated to the level of deputy commanders. Surya was designated as the 'nayaka', head of the naval force. Rajendra Chola thought he would make him the jalathipathy in a few years. Right now, he did not want to upset the generals who were senior to him in years of service. *We should consider performance and not the passive years of service for promotions,* he thought. One day he would build up this feature in his governance philosophy. But he wanted to introduce this gradually so that the seniors did not get upset.

Nagapattinam was decorated, people were celebrating. The sounds of drums and trumpets could be heard even when the ship was in the high seas. The town wore a festive look, rightfully so, since the flags of the Chola kingdom were flying far and wide even on the shores beyond the sea.

Every citizen was proud of their Chola lineage. They were all wearing the pride of their nation on their sleeves. They were dancing and singing with gusto.

Rajendra Chola got down from the ship with his deputies amidst the sounds of the Vedic hymns chanted by pandits and the beating of drums and other musical instruments. The queens applied tilaks on his face. The palace was illuminated and decorated. After spending a few hours with his son, Rajathi Raja and getting a briefing on the matters relating to the state, Rajendra Chola rested.

The new queen was received by the other queens who were curiously looking at her, as her features were different from theirs. The young queen had a yellowish red complexion with beautiful features. There was an element of jealousy creeping among the queens, as they expected the king would spend more time with the princess of Srivijaya kingdom.

The king spent the next few weeks with the young beautiful princess. For a moment, the king doubted whether he was a right match for this young lady. But the princess of Srivijaya mesmerized him with her abundant love and affection. Rajendra Chola mostly kept indoors for the next few months.

Soon the ruler held a review meeting with his officials.

'Minister, Krishna Raman, I have to make Rajathi Raja Chola my co-regent. Let him take charge. I want to spend time on the construction of Gangaikonda Cholapuram. I see security lapses in Thanjavur.

'People from various countries came during the construction of the temple during my father's time and permanently settled here. We find it difficult to keep our big military stationed here. During the monsoon, crossing the Cauvery River and its tributaries to get to the north with all our elephants and horses takes more time and energy. We need to move out. I want to make Gangaikonda Cholapuram our capital and on the same day, formally crown myself with the royal crown and regal jewels, we reclaimed from Srivijaya.

Moreover, on the same day I will declare my son Rajathi Raja Chola as my co-regent.'

'Good thought, Your Majesty. For the review of the progress of the new city, Keerthi, come here to explain.'

'Keerthi, my Vishvakarma, how are you? Despite objections from my ministers I chose you. Hope you will not let me down.'

'Your Majesty, we are nearing completion. In a month's time we can have your coronation as Emperor Mummudhi Chola (Mummudhi Chola means the king of the Cheras, Cholas and Pandyas) with the newly won royal crown in this new city.'

'As far as the Choleswara temple is concerned, I do not involve myself much since Gunavan, the sculptor and creator of the temple, does not like others to interfere.'

71

Gunavan the chief architect of the Choleswara temple was trained by Kunjaran, chief architect of the Brihadishvara temple, built by his father.

'Gunavan, you are aware, during the final stage of the construction of the Brihadishvara temple, some sculptures were left unfinished. That is because that sculptor did not want to work on any statue which my father could not see.

'I do not want such a scenario to arise in the new temple constructed by me. I want everything to be completed during my life. So please expedite.'

'Yes, Your Majesty, in a few months' time everything will be ready.'

'I want to have the inauguration of the city during the forthcoming Sadhya Vizha (the birth anniversary of King Raja Raja Chola).

With this, the meeting was over. They made the following key resolutions.

- By Sadhya Vizha, the new city will be dedicated to the public and the Chola capital will get shifted.
- Crown Prince Rajathi Raja will become a co-regent on the same day.
- There will be a new coronation of King Rajendra Chola as Emperor Mummudhi Cholan. He will wear the Pandya royal crown, mythical aaram and the

garland of precious pearls captured from the Srivijaya kingdom.

While the meeting got over, Surya came to pay respects to the king.

'Pranam, Your Majesty. Hope you have rested well and keepig good health with the blessings of Lord Brihadishvara.'

'Everything is fine, Surya. When is your child expected? How is Luli? What are you doing these days?'

'Your Majesty, my wife is expected to deliver anytime. As for me, I do not have any challenges these days. We have no wars forthcoming immediately. I need challenges.'

'I understand Surya. You always need more challenges. Now I give you the additional charge of creating the new city spy network.'

'We have fixed the date for the inauguration. It is due to be held in the next month. It is not far off. I want you to set up a new strong spy network. Many foreigners come here. We have no identification tag system as followed by the kingdom of Krishna in ancient Dwarka. Many bad elements may exploit this new capital city. Our minister Raman heads the national spy network, but I need a special one for the capital. I want you to take this additional portfolio, apart from your Chola navy assignments.'

'Thank you, Your Majesty, my plate will be full. You have given me more than what I asked for.'

While Surya was discussing this, he got the message that his wife just delivered a boy baby. His joy was uncontrollable.

The Chola ruler gifted him with diamond jewels and congratulated him.

Surya said, 'I am going to name him Jala Raja, as he was born immediately after our naval expedition to Srivijaya.'

72

Surya soon commenced his new assignment. He made a couple of trips to the new city under construction with Gujili. He missed Ajili.

As far as the spy network was concerned, he did not want to add manpower, as he wanted total secrecy. Hence, his new deportment included himself and Gujili.

He met Keerthi a couple of times. Once he accidentally saw a message-carrying bird at his house. He was left wondering whether Keerthi used these pigeons for sharing messages.

With whom was he sharing messages? Did he have connections with his Lankan king, Mahinda, in jail? He always had some doubts about Keerthi. Since he had travelled with him up to Rohana, to meet Mahinda in hiding, he knew a little bit about his personality. *When he could easily turn against his own king in a fraction of a second, he cannot be reliable,* he thought. But Keerthi's skill for creating new cities made him dear to Rajendra Chola.

Surya decided to increase his surveillance on Keerthi and Mahinda. He decided to use Gujili to intercept the pigeon, when it was flying towards Keerthi's house.

The plan worked. Gujili intercepted a message from the pigeon carrying the message to Keerthi. Instead, he left blank silk cloths as a message to confuse Keerthi.

The intercepted message was opened by Surya. 'Meet me at Chudamani' was the message. It was signed by Vajrabahu.

Surya wondered who he was. He could make out that Chudamani was the vihara in Nagapattinam. The vihara was not in the spy network radar, as it was headed by the ruler's sister, Madevadigal.

Surya took permission from Luli and moved to Nagapattinam. Before leaving, he planted sweet kisses on Jala Raja and his beautiful, caring wife.

73

Nagapattinam

The rising sun with the backdrop of the sea was a beautiful sight. The sandy beach was full of people even during the morning.

The traders of different nationalities were busy making their deals. Horses from Arabia, colourful birds from Srivijaya, silk from China were articles getting offloaded at the port. On the other side, spices, rice and grains were getting loaded.

Surya looked at the Chudamani Vihara, facing the sea. Many Buddhist saints of different ages lived here. Daily prayers were held. Young monks from Lanka, Srivijaya, Kalinga were all trained here. Surya changed his attire, shaved off his hair, removed his moustache and wore a Buddhist monk's robe.

He went in as a young monk seeking salvation.

While attending a prayer session Surya noticed that there was a huge Buddha golden statue that came from the Srivijaya kingdom but surprisingly the Buddha wore a black crown and necklace with black stone jewellery. It looked strange on him—the combination of yellow and black metal on a Buddha statue? *May be it is something unique*, he thought.

People from different walks of life assembled at the prayer hall. The head monk and the deputy head nun were leading the prayers. The head monk looked more like a warrior. He had a rather unpleasant face with a number of scars all over it. It seemed he was not at peace with himself. He was continuously upset with his supporting monks. He was restless.

Surya's attention was drawn towards his sharp powerful eyes, which he had seen somewhere. But he could not recollect.

Then his attention turned to the nun. *She was a fifty-year-old lady, must be a seasoned saint*, he thought.

The morning prayer session resounding with '*Buddham Saranam Gacchami*' was followed by a lecture by the monk and then by the nun. He came to know from a new trainee monk that the head monk was Vajrabahu and the nun Nivedita.

Surya was surveying the the prayer hall. His mind was not on the lecture. But suddenly something said in the lecture got his attention.

74

'Welcome new trainee-monks. Students from the Lanka, Srivijaya, Chera, Chola and Pandya kingdoms.'

'Life is full of miseries. Why? This is because of our desire. Hence, kill the desire which is the root cause of all problems.

'Take my case. I had a good royal life in Lanka, loved a person so dear to me, but he ditched me for reasons best known to him after giving me a child.

'I was jailed due to certain lapses of my husband, not due to any fault of mine. I gave birth to my son at the Rameswaram jail.

'But I denounced my desire and moved away from my husband and my son. Devoid of desire, I adopted Buddhism. After wandering for a while after my release, I came here as a trainee-monk like you.

'My soul became peaceful, and with that inner peace, I am happy to train new monks.

'I destroyed my desire, adapted to Buddhism, so I am peaceful today.'

The lecture shook Surya. *She is my biological mother. Neither my biological father whom I met at Srivijaya nor my adopted father could locate her whereabouts. At last I had found her. But let me keep it as a secret for now and see what will happen...*' Surya thought.

He retired to his house he had rented at the port city and decided to carry out more surveillance over the Chudamani Vihara.

One day Surya saw the message-carrying pigeon flying towards Chudamani Vihara. Gujili intercepted it, and a message was extracted from its body. The message read: 'Are royal crown and regal jewels safe?' It was signed by none other than Keerthi. It was addressed to Vajrabahu.

Oh my God, my suspicions came true. But why do they raise this settled subject of the regal jewels captured from Srivijaya? What is happening? Surya was confused and tried to seek answers.

He decided to replace the message. 'Are the royal crown and the jewels safe with you? Where are they? The Cholas claim to have conquered them from Srivijaya', and the pigeon was released. Surya was waiting for the reply. As expected, the pigeon returned with the message. He checked it and was rather shocked when he read it.

75

The message from Vajrabahu read: 'The regal jewels are safe. All these are painted black and are placed on a Buddha statue in the vihara. The Cholas captured the jewels that are fake and planted by us at Lanka.'

My goodness, how have they cheated us?! Surya thought. *The grand coronation date was fixed. It is just a week away. We have to do something. But how?* Surya thought.

A few days passed by. He had to go to Gangaikonda Cholapuram to oversee the arrangements of the function.

He thought of alerting the ruler. But it would be terrible if he delayed the function for the grand coronation. He just informed his ruler about the duplicate jewels and told him that he would go after the parties involved in this scheme and come back to the grand coronation with the original regal jewels on time. He requested that no one should be informed as it would create panic. He would not take any action against the suspects immediately but would go with the flow and catch all the culprits behind such scheming. Till then, he would only exchange messages through Gujili. With this message shared with his ruler, Surya departed for Gangaikonda Cholapuram along with Gujili.

Countdown to the grand coronation of Emperor Rajendra Chola

The new city was getting ready for the occasion. Surya went around it and was mesmerized by its grand design. It was the city created to commemorate the Chola victory over the Pala dynasty and the Ganga belt. It was an extensive city, carefully planned to suit the needs of a capital.

The city had two fortifications, one inner and the other outer. The outer was wider and built from burnt bricks and was about 6 to 8 feet wide. It consisted of two walls, the intervening space (the core) being filled with sand. The bricks were fairly large in size and made of well-burnt clay.

The outer fortification was called Rajendra Chola Madil. The inner fortification was around the royal palace. The mammoth royal palace was built of burnt brick. The ceilings were covered with flat tiles of small size in fine lime mortar. The pillars were made of polished wood supported on granite bases.

There was both wet and dry land inside the fort used for cultivation and other purposes. With the palace at the centre of the city, towards the northeast (ishanya) was the great Shiva temple.

Then he came to the Choleswara temple. Its basement had

an 80-feet foundation. The tower was initially planned for 214 feet, but Rajendra Chola ordered to reduce the height to 186 feet, as he did not want to construct a tower taller than the one created by his father in Thanjavur.

But he permitted a taller murti (statue) of 13 feet tall that was dressed in a nine-yard-long cloth. Sculptures depicting Shaivite philosophy were all over the temple.

Some of the exquisite sculptures brought from the Ganga expedition of Rajendra Chola were also placed in the temple. The sun was depicted as a lotus spreading its petals, a unique feature of this temple.

The Nataraja statue would smile at you when seen from any direction. The sculptures looked like living entities.

The sanctum sanctorum was pasted with chandra kanda stones on its walls to provide heat during cold months and keep it cool it during summer. The temple wall was six hundred feet tall and 450 feet wide. Just on the right side of Nandi, there was a well with a lion face. It was filled with water from the Ganges. There was an underground tunnel that linked the temple and the palace.

Inside the temple there were big halls standing with the support of 140 pillars. Surya could not control his excitement on seeing the grand temple.

There were a number of ponds, small tanks and wells to supply drinking water. There was an irrigation canal, Madurantaka Vadavaru, east of the capital city.

The entryways were named Thiruvasal, (the eastern gate) and Vembugudi, evidently the south gate leading to the village Vembugudi situated in that direction. Highways were named after Raja Raja Chola and Rajendra Chola as Rajarajan Peruvali and Rajendran Peruvali respectively. The streets included the ten streets (pattu teru), the gateway lane (thiruvasal narasam) and the Suddhamali lane. The other highways were Thirumadil Peruvali, Vilangudaiyan Peruvali and Kulaiyanai Pora Peruvali (the highway through which the palace elephant passed by). As Surya moved with great excitement, he stopped at the grand new lake Gangapuri.

77

The mammoth lake was called the liquid pillar of victory (Jalamayam Jaya Sthambham) and housed water brought from the Ganga River.

It was the largest man-made lake in the region created by Rajendra Chola. Surya thought of swimming in it and so jumped right into it. To his surprise he saw a small closed hall underwater. The hall had many poles constructed above the ceiling.

These poles had their openings above the water. The openings were huge. Surya understood that the air was being circulated to the underwater hall through these multiple poles. The poles or jalasthambas were coloured. Surya wondered, *Does anybody know about a hall under the water? Why do we need a secret hall under the water?*

As these questions crossed the mind of Surya, he observed that the hall was connected by an underwater tunnel. He swam above the tunnel and found that it led to the main palace hall where the grand coronation was to be held. Again, multiple openings through the poles were providing air circulation to these tunnels.

For outsiders, these poles were jalasthambas. But these pillars provided air circulation to the secret underground water palace and tunnel. *A brilliant design*, he thought. Then he recalled that the Rohana palace with underwater secrets. He did realize Keerthi, the minister who constructed this city was the same man who created the Rohana water palace. He was a champion of water engineering.

'But does our ruler Rajendra Chola know this or is it kept away from his knowledge?' Surya was confused.

A couple of days were left for the grand coronation. He heard Keerthi was staying in the new city. He thought of taking him head-on. He had to act fast.

He rushed to Keerthi's place. The pigeon messenger was waiting outside Keerthi's place. Surya acted immediately.

78

Before the pigeon could reach Keerthi, Surya took the message attached to its body. He saw the message: 'Everyone is meeting at the jala palace at Chola Ganga tonight. Let the palace underground passage be kept open after sunset.'

It was a message from Vajrabahu to Keerthi. Upon reading this message, Surya attached the message back to the pigeon. He wanted Keerthi to read it so that the plan could be carried out. That alone would enable Surya to catch all the culprits red-handed.

Surya's anxiety levels shot up. He had four nazhigas for the sun to set. He got ready. Surya kept his eyes and ears close to the underwater hall.

He went inside the tunnel, sat in one of the inner sides of the pillar. He could get a clear view of what was happening from there. He could also clearly listen to conversations. He was ready and waiting.

After sunset, the secret underwater hall witnessed some activity. In very little time the hall was full. *Who has assembled here?* Surya was curious.

Keerthi; Ulang Kiu the new queen of the Srivijaya kingdom; Vajrabahu, the Buddhist monk; Nivedita, the Buddhist nun, were all present there. In addition, there were three men—one looked like a Chera Brahmin by his hairstyle, the other looked like a Lankan and the third was a dark-skinned man who spoke in Tamil and appeared to be from Pandya desam.

Keerthi addressed the gathering:

'We are now at the last phase of our agenda. It is time to finish our task tomorrow at sunrise. The grand coronation starts as soon as the sun rises. We have only limited time left. Now each of you introduce your grievance in your own words, as we are all meeting together for the first and last time today.'

Keerthi stated, 'King Mahinda was tortured, the Cholas looted us for three generations. We cannot win a war against them. We have to defeat them by proxy war schemes only. That is why I waited for ten long years for striking at the right time. Now the time has arrived.'

Ulang Kiu added, 'My father, King of Srivijaya, got me married to a man who was sixty years old. He may be an emperor but he cannot even meet my biological needs. He cannot even give me children. My sister Tunga Devi escaped and joined our enemy camp at Savaga Island. She may revolt against the Cholas. So I want to get rid of him before she does.'

Nivedita said, 'I am the sister of the deposed queen of Lanka who was captured as a prisoner along with King Mahinda. I escaped from being raped. I want to hit back the Cholas strongly. This is the moment for me.'

Another Brahmin man who could not be identified by Surya joined in. He said, 'I am Kalidasa, son of Ravi Dasa, who was charged with the murder of Rajendra Chola's uncle Aditya Karikala. My father and the Chera Brahmin families were driven out of this kingdom by Rajendra Chola's father, depriving us all of our assets. I am eagerly waiting this great moment.'

The other man added, 'I am Kassappa, son of Mahinda, the Lankan king in the Cholas' jail for twelve long years. I was brought up secretively in the jungles of Lanka. I want to seize this moment, kill the Chola ruler and release my father, mother and my sister.'

The dark-skinned man said, 'I am Amarabujanga Pandya. After I was defeated, I live in the jungles of the mountain like an animal. I want to get back to my treasures, captured by the Cholas.'

79

Vajrabahu removed his mask. He looked like the former ruler Raja Raja Chola. The eyes were just like his, Surya could see from close quarters. He recalled that his eyes got registered in his mind, even during his first visit to the Chudamani Vihara.

Surya listened carefully: 'All of you may be seeing me for the first time. I have a long history of enmity with Rajendra Chola. Raja Raja Chola was wandering all over Chola Mandala, when his uncle Uthama Chola was ruling the kingdom. He spent some time in Lanka also. At that time, he fell in love with Bama Devi, a commoner working in the palace. He had sexual union with her and promised to marry her, once he was back to the Chola capital city. He went back, became a king under dramatic circumstances. Bama Devi gave birth to me and died. I only have the ring given by King Raja Raja Chola to my mother.

'I was never able to reach even the gates of the palace. I grew up as a boy not knowing my father's name, ridiculed as a bastard. I felt humiliated. I decided to take on Rajendra Chola. Had I not been born out of wedlock, I would have been the heir apparent, as I am older to him. I captured their vessel carrying their treasures, but one of the Chola commanders made me forcibly stay in the far-off Srivijaya kingdom. From there, I escaped and stayed in the Chola kingdom as a Buddhist monk. My moment has arrived now.'

Surya recalled his father's reference to someone who

may threaten the Chola monarchy. He refused to divulge the details. He was working on a mission of locating this man who escaped from his surveillance. So he could not enter the Chola kingdom. Alas, his father died without accomplishing his mission.

When they all completed their grievances, Vajrabahu came out with the plan. 'Now we have three hours left for the commencement of the grand coronation.'

'We can all reach the coronation hall from here through the underground tunnel, very ably created by Keerthi. Please note this plan. The coronation hall was guarded by all our men. Those who came from the Lanka, Pandya and Chera kingdoms for the palace work, were assembled by Keerthi. The city security was also with Keerthi. The pandits from the Chera kingdom were loyal to us. They were all from the lineage of Ravi Dasa, the Chera Brahmin driven away by Rajendra Chola's father.

'The royal crown and the regal jewels currently in the possession of Rajendra Chola are all fake. Long ago, I took these away to Srivijaya at the request of the deposed Lankan king, Mahinda. He deliberately placed fake jewels as the real ones. Rajendra Chola will be killed during the coronation. I will not reveal how, as I keep that secret till the very end. There will be chaos.

'In this melee, I will enter with the royal crown and regal jewels to claim my rights to throne as the son of Raja Raja Chola. I will claim that these regal jewels were given to me by Raja Raja Chola to prove my lineage. You will all support my move, I will become the ruler. Then we will all share this kingdom.'

What a cunning plan? All the disgruntled elements have

assembled here, Surya thought.

He had three hours left. He wanted to send the message to Soman, his first leader, the Lankan regional Chola commander, who was taking care of the security arrangements of the ruler at the coronation hall. But he did not know whether he was reliable. Surya started doubting everyone. He sent the message first to the king through Gujili. Again, he sent the same message to Soman. But how did they plan to kill the ruler? This was still not known.

Who could be the killer? What could be the method? Surya had to act. Only three hours were left for the coronation.

80

Surya used all his special skills. He walked on the water from pole to pole standing on the ceilings of the underwater halls and tunnels. He pierced holes, cut those poles, so that the water flowed inside the underwater halls and tunnels. The underwater hall and tunnels were soon flooded. It was a sudden flow of water and all the inmates inside the underwater space died on the spot as they couldn't breathe.

The jalastumbas created a jala samadhi, the enemies of the Chola kingdom were vanquished. The Chola Ganga absorbed those evil souls under it. They all stayed buried forever.

There was a sigh of relief for Surya. But he had to stop the attempt to kill his ruler. He had only an hour left. He ran on the water to cross the lake to reach the coronation hall.

When he reached the hall he surveyed the security outside. He saw nothing unusual.

As he entered the coronation hall, the crowning of the emperor was about to start. He must nab the killer. Who could he be?

81

The Grand Coronation

At sunrise on Sadhya Vizha day Vedic hymns were heard all over the coronation hall, which was full of people. Security was very tight. Sounds of Vedic hymns reverberated in the hall.

> *Om Try-Ambakam Yajaamahe*
> *Sugandhim Pusstti-Vardhanam*
> *Urvaarukam-Iva Bandhanaan*
> *Mrtyor-Mukssiiya Maa-[A]mrtaat*

We worship the Three-Eyed One (Lord Shiva),
Who is fragrant (spiritual essence) and
Who nourishes all beings.
May He sever our bondage of Samsara (worldly life),
like a cucumber (severed from the bondage of its creeper),
And thus liberate us from the fear of death,
By making us realize that we are never separated
from our Immortal Nature.

Offerings were made to eight deities—Savita, Agni, Soma, Brahaspati, Indra, Rudra, Mitra and Varuna.

Savita was invoked for righteous energy of the king, Agni for mastery of the household, Soma for protection of forests and agriculture, Brahaspati for power of speech, Indra for supremacy in matters of administration, Rudra for protection of cattle, Mitra for truth and Varuna for upholding dharma or law. Thus each sobriquet denotes one duty of the king.

After the homa (sacrifice) to these deities was over, the king sat on a tiger's skin and was blessed with an invincible life, obedient subjects and a strong kingdom, by sprinkling holy water from the sacred rivers Saraswati, Ganga, Narmada, Sindhu and Cauvery; a sea; a whirlpool; a pond; a well and the dew. In this water, flavoured powder and Durva grass were mixed. The sprinkling was made by a Brahmin priest, reciting Vedic hymns.

Rajendra Chola was bathed with this water. Then the ruler wore new clothes with glittering jewels embedded on them. Rajendra Chola then took three steps forward, symbolically to represent the subjugation of the religion, repeating for each act a separate mantra. The priest in the meantime offered an oblation to the fire with the agnidhara collecting a portion of the water that had run over the deities at the time of abhishek (offering).

After this, the king was seated on the throne. The priest touched the chest of the ruler and asked him to recite, 'I will uphold the sacred law and order'.

The priest then moved to hand over the sword as a symbol of royal power and military strength. The sword is symbolic of Indra's thunderbolt.

The ruler then announced various awards and rewards to the generals. Minister Krishna Raman conferred various titles on the ruler, who becomes an emperor from that day. Alongside, the crown prince was conferred the title of co-regent. Krishna Raman announced, 'Jayasimha Sarabhan (vanquisher of Jayasimha), Mannaikonda Cholan (the king, who took possession of Mannai or Manyakheta the Chalukyas), above all Mummudhi Cholan (ruler of the Cheras, Cholas and Pandyas). Vijayee Bhava. Long live the emperor!'

As that point Surya entered in a hurry. He saw nothing unusual. But he knew something was going to happen. But what?

At that moment, Emperor Rajendra Chola was about to be crowned with the Pandya royal crown, garlanded with the mythical aaram and the precious pearl garlands captured from the Srivijaya kingdom.

Surya saw the Chera Brahmin with his typical Chera-type tuft moving towards the emperor with the royal crown. There was a spark in his brain. Ravi Dasa's son was talking about murdering the ruler. *He must be the murderer.* The Chera Bramhin was slowly starting to climb the podium on which the emperor was sitting. His one hand was balancing the crown on a platter and the other moving towards his waist.

Surya sprang into action. He covered the distance between the first few rows of courtiers and bounded up the steps. His actions made the royal guards nervous who started to converge around the king while two of them started towards Surya. The Chera Brahmin sensing something amiss quickly reacted and started to run towards the emperor. Pretending as if he was afraid he let the crown slip and in a desperate attempt took the dagger out.

It was as if time was in slow motion for Surya. He saw himself close to the attacker but was helpless to stop his attack. He did the unthinkable—almost as a last attempt to stop the Brahmin, he threw himself in between the emperor and the attacker. The dagger aimed towards the emperor's chest descended in a swift blow and caught Surya in his neck. Surya saw that his desperate attempt had worked. The attack was stopped, and the Brahmin stumbled under his own momentum. As blood gushed out of his throat, Surya started to lose his senses as darkness started to cloud his vision. His mind flashed with the pictures of his wife and boy, but his smile was reserved for the picture of his emperor rushing forward to his assistance.

The dagger was tipped with poison. Surya convulsed a couple of times and died on the spot. He had bravely given up his life by saving his emperor and safeguarding his country's future. The whole hall was stunned by the turn of the events.

82

Emperor Rajendra Chola closed the eyes of Surya and gave a fitting tribute to the martyr, the great marine warrior.

'All of you do not know what a great service Surya rendered to our Chola kingdom. He detected the evil designs of our enemies, the Lankans, Pandyas, Chera Brahmins and Srivijayans, who were bent on carrying out the cowardly act of destroying our kingdom by killing me. Having lost the wars with us, they waged proxy wars. I will single out two people in that group, who were never reckoned in our enemy list. One is a Lankan-born warrior, who claims to be fathered by my father Raja Raja Chola. He sat there in the Chudamani Vihara right in our kingdom, as a Buddhist monk and planned the cunning schemes.

'His claim of my father's lineage is questionable and could be a part of the evil designs of the Lankan who lost the wars.

'The next surprising person in the enemy list is none other than the Srivijaya princess who married me, in accordance with the wishes of her father who lost the war with us. She tried to unseat me and create chaos in our kingdom so that Srivijaya could rise again.

'Let us erase these two from our history. No inscription or no writing should cover them as a part of our history. Let our future generations not know about the existence of these people during our era.

'Now all the visible and invisible enemies, planning a coup

in a secret hall under the Chola Ganga water were completely destroyed by Surya on time. All our enemies stay buried forever under Chola Ganga.

'They tried to keep the real royal crown and the regal jewels by making us chase the fake ones. But a timely detection by Surya enabled me to replace those real ones placed on the Buddha statue by the fake ones which came to us. We could do this on time, without the enemy knowing about our act.

'My sister Madevadigal, who is the overall head of the Chudamani Vihara assisted me to replace these fake ones with the real ones lying in the vihara. Between religious loyalty and national loyalty, she stood for the nation, our Chola kingdom. Our pranams to her.

'We lost one of our greatest warriors. I wished on his graduation ceremony that he should become our jalathipathy. After he won the Srivijaya kingdom, I should have given him the title of jalathipathy. But I delayed it since I thought such a gesture will upset the seniors.

'I declare from now on, it will be performance and not age that will determine promotions in our Chola kingdom. This will become the new norm of our governance henceforth.

'Surya will always be the jalathipathy of our navy for generations.

'I appoint Luli as our ambassador to Srivijaya and Kamboja.

'Surya will be given full state honours and our flags will fly at half-mast for a month. We will give him a celebrated cremation that is given for a ruler. Long live Jalathipathy Surya's memories!'

'I crown him with this royal crown and regal jewels which he captured single-handedly. Let Surya be cremated with all these regal jewels. He is the one who truly deserves these. I do not want to wear these.

'Long live, Surya!'

The emperor's voice broke, tears rolled down everyone's eyes.

The wandering soul of the great warrior Surya, who was killed by a pandit will be reborn in a Brahmin family as a warrior in AD 1500, supporting Hemu, the Brahmin ruler.

Epilogue

A few decades later, Surya's son Jala Raja supported by Suryavarman, the king of Kamboja, built one of the greatest wonders of the world—Angkor Wat. It was a tribute he paid to the Chola kingdom by showcasing Chola sculpture and art to the world. The great monument stands till date.

Acknowledgements

At the outset, I have to thank the Almighty for kindling my passion to write. What did not occur to me in the past few decades, suddenly arose in my mind as a spark one morning. The spark lit flames of unbridled passion in me.

I register my gratitude to my think-tank. Its dynamic members with youth and exuberance tolerated my constant intrusion into their personal time. They supported me in perfecting the core story, ensuring the smooth flow of the narrative and promoting the book.

The key members of this think-tank who walked along with me shoulder to shoulder on this project are Padmanabh Diwanji (Paddy) from the UAE and Priyanka Durgadoss and Jyothsna Durgadoss from California.

There were others who relentlessly assisted me in terms of the research, conversion of manuscripts into digital files and taking the role of critics. They include Vijayakumaran (UAE), Vijoy Joseph (UAE) and Hemal Vyaa (UAE).

I am grateful to Kapish Mehra, managing director, Rupa Publications for showing confidence in this book and taking the series forward. The assistance we got from Dibakar Ghosh, editorial director and legal head was invaluable. He and his team have worked hard to polish the manuscript and get it to the publication stage.

I would like to register my gratitude to Madhav Menon (UAE), whose enthusiastic guidance from day one helped to convert my dream into reality. He was instrumental in helping me reach the right publisher.

A special thanks is conveyed to my media partner IBD (India) Pvt Ltd, represented by Rajagopal and Karthi for giving me a 24/7 promotional support. I also thank the promotion and distribution team of my publishers.

Above all, I could not have spent quality time on this project, but for the support of my wife Gowri Durgadoss. In addition, I owe my gratitude to Suresh Bhatia and Rajeev Bhatia (UAE), the businessmen who support me in every project of mine.

Further, I thank all those who follow me on Facebook, Twitter, YouTube, Google Plus, my blog and my website.

The book relies on a vast body of research by a large number of scholars. I thank all these sources.

Finally, I register my debt of gratitude to all my well-wishers.

Glossary

Aaram	A necklace.
Agnidhara	An assistant to pandits.
Amavasya	The new moon day in the Hindu calendar.
Anuradhapura	Ancient kingdom in modern-day Sri Lanka.
Brihadishvara	Brihadishvara temple, also called Rajarajesvaram temple or Peruvudaiyar Kovil, is a Hindu temple dedicated to Lord Shiva located in Thanjavur, Tamil Nadu. It is one of the largest South Indian temples and an exemplary example of fully realized Tamil architecture.
Buddham Saranam Gacchami	A ritual chant in Buddhism meaning 'I take refuge in the Buddha'.
Chakravyuha	A circular military formation tough to penetrate.
Chamakam	A hymn for Lord Rudra and some of the most revered chants and mantras.
Chandra kanda	Moonstone, a semi-precious stone.
Chera kingdom	Present-day Kerala.
Chinese Song dynasty	The Song dynasty era began in AD 960 and continued until AD 1279. It controlled China proper and southern China.
Chitradurga	Chitradurga is a city and the headquarters of Chitradurga district which is located in Karnataka.

Chola kingdom	One of the largest and successful empires in India. At its peak it controlled areas from the Maldives Islands to the Malay peninsula.
Chudamani Vihara	Chudamani Vihara is an ancient Buddhist monstery in Nagapattinam, Tamil Nadu. Chudamani Vihara was constructed in AD 1006 by the Srivijayan king Sri Vijaya Maravijayattungavarman under the patronage of Raja Raja Chola.
Dhandabukti	A marshy kingdom that was situated between modern-day Odisha and West Bengal.
Datta homam	A Vedic ritual for formalizing the adoption of children in Vedic times.
Drishadvati	Drishadvati River is hypothesized by Indologists to identify the route of the Vedic river Saraswati and the state of Brahmavarta. According to Manusmriti, Brahmavarta, where the rishis composed the Vedas and other texts of the Vedic religion, was at the confluence of the Saraswati and Drishadvati.
Eethi	A spike or a spear.
Gotra	In Hindu society, the term 'gotra' is considered to be equivalent to clan. It broadly refers to people who are descendants in an unbroken male line from a common male ancestor.
Guru Drona	Guru Droṇa or Rajaguru Devadrona was the royal preceptor to the Kauravas

	and the Pandavas. He was a master of advanced military arts, including the divine weapons or astras.
Gurukul	A system of education prevalent in ancient India whereby children stayed with their teacher to gain knowledge.
Ilamuridesam	A kingdom that existed in the same place as modern-day Sumatra, Indonesia.
Ishanya	Northeast direction
Jai Vijaye Bhava	May you be victorious.
Jala samadhi	Literally means, the final resting place is in the water. Or buried underwater.
Jalasthambas	Literally means, a pillar in the water.
Jalathipathy	Commander of the navy.
Jannantha	The northern kingdom of Polonnaruwa that was renamed Mangalam.
Kailasha	A mountain in the Himalayan range supposed to the abode of Lord Shiva.
Kaliyuga	The last of the four yugas or epochs in the Hindu timeline. The Kaliyuga is marked by a rise in injustice and a fall in the righteousness and religiosity of people.
Kanni	A tactical formation used in the Chola navy.
Katar	A push dagger used in close combat.
Kuru War	Also known as the Kurukshetra or Mahabharata War.
Kuthuval	A short sword.
Lemuri	The kingdom of Ilamuridesam (Lemuri) also known as Lamuri approximately covered the present Aceh province of the

	island Sumatra. It was a kingdom under Srivijaya empire, named after the capital city.
Lakshmi Ganapati homam	A Vedic religious ritual that is performed for Lord Ganpati to remove all the obstacles and negative energies and give victory or success, acquire good health, wealth and prosperity.
Lord Muruga	Also known as Lord Kartikeya. He is the Hindu Rashtrakuta god of war.
Madil	A wall.
Mahmud of Ghazni	Mahmud of Ghazni was the most prominent ruler of the Ghaznavid empire. He conquered the eastern Iranian lands, modern Afghanistan and the northwestern Indian subcontinent (modern Pakistan) from AD 997 to his death in AD 1030.
Mullaitivu	A province in northern Sri Lanka. A district by the same name continues to be present today.
Nazhiga	Twenty-four minutes equal one nazhiga.
Oddha Desha	Modern-day Odisha.
Pancha bhootas	The pancha bootas are the five elemements: vayu (air), agni (fire), jal (water) and prithvi (earth).
Podigaimalai	The Pothigai Hills, also known as the Shiva Jothi Parvath, Agasthiyar Mountain, Southern Kailash are in the southern part of the Western Ghats. Ancient tradition holds the mountains of Pothigai to be where the sage Agastiyar (Akattiyan)

	provided the first grammar for the Tamil language.
Polonnaruwa	Polonnaruwa is the main town of Polonnaruwa district in North Central Province, Sri Lanka.
Raj dharma	Raj dharma means the duty of the rulers, which was intrinsically entwined with the concept of bravery and Kshatriya dharma. In another interpretation, it guides the individual to incorporate spirituality in his/her work life and in his personal life.
Rashtrakuta	A kingdom and dynasty that was strong in the central and western regions of India from AD 7 to 10 centuries.
Rig Veda	Rig Veda is the first of the four vedas, the sacred texts of hinduism. The Rig Veda is an ancient Indian text collection that compiles vedic hymns and verses dedicated to Vedic deities. Together with Yajur Veda, Sama Veda and Atharva Veda, the Rig Veda is one of the four canonical sacred texts of Hinduism, known collectively as the Vedas.
Rudram	It is one of the most sacred and powerful mantras found in Krishna Yajur Veda.
Ruhuna	A place in southern Sri Lanka.
Sadhya Vizha	Sadhya is a star of the day when Emperor Raja Raja Chola was born. The Sadhya Viza literally means the evening of the sadhya—a star.

Sama Veda	The Sama Veda is the Veda of melodies and chants.
Senathipathy	Chief of an armed force.
Shaivism	It is one of the major traditions in Hinduism that reveres Lord Shiva as the Supreme Being. The followers of Shaivism are called Shaivites.
Srivijaya	Srivijaya was a dominant Malay city-state based on the island of Sumatra, Indonesia, which influenced much of Southeast Asia. Srivijaya was an important centre for the expansion of Buddhism from the 8th to the 12th centuries.
Sunga Illaka	The customs and excise arm of the Chola navy.
Vimana	The spire of a temple.
Vriksham	A tree.